"What are you up to this time, Marti?"

Farrell stormed into her room uninvited, and his vitality filled the air. "A few bruises from a little riding and you suddenly want to miss dinner! Is it all becoming too much for you?"

"No, I just felt tired, and—"

"Wanted to be alone again so you could wallow in more self-pity, is that it?"

"You consider I have cause to, then?" Marti countered weakly.

"No, but if you're short on reasons, maybe this will help!" Farrell pulled her into his arms and kissed her long and hard.

Marti broke free and railed at him. "Get out of here, Farrell! And don't you ever do that again!"

"Well, at least I succeeded in getting you firing on all four cylinders again," he drawled lazily. "And I think I prefer you fiery."

Kerry Allyne developed wanderlust after emigrating with her family from England to Australia. A long working holiday enabled her to travel the world before returning to Australia where she met her engineer husband-to-be. After marriage and the birth of two children, the family headed north to Summerland, a popular surfing resort, where they run a small cattle farm and an electrical contracting business. Kerry Allyne's travel experience adds much to the novels she spends her days writing—when, that is, she's not doing company accounts or herding cattle!

Books by Kerry Allyne

The Tullagindi Rodeo

Kerry Allyne

Harlequin Books

TORONTO • NEW YORK • LONDON
AMSTERDAM • PARIS • SYDNEY • HAMBURG
STOCKHOLM • ATHENS • TOKYO • MILAN

Original hardcover edition published in 1986
by Mills & Boon Limited

ISBN 0-373-02809-1

Harlequin Romance first edition January 1987

CHAPTER ONE

MARTINE GRAYSON stared at her father incredulously as he sat propped against the pillows of the king-sized bed he occupied in the spacious and expensively decorated master bedroom of their substantial Brisbane home.

'The Tullagindi Rodeo!' she expostulated in a mixture of disbelief and derision at his request—no, order! she amended with silent resentment—for her to attend that annual event in his stead this particular year, due to his inability to do so because he was still convalescing from a recent, though only minor, operation. 'You can't be serious! You know the outback has never held any interest for me, and if it comes to that, why on earth does one of us have to attend, anyway?' And without giving him time to reply, 'Oh, I know you always make a point of going each year in order to keep in touch with the area and the people you grew up with—' even after forty years spent in the city making a not inconsiderable fortune, he was still nothing if not a true representation of the old saying that, 'you can take the boy out of the bush, but you can't take the bush out of the boy' '—but apart from my having absolutely no desire to go, I very much doubt I'd make much of a substitute for you, and I'm just as certain no one there would think so either.'

'While I'm equally sure they will be most happy to see you, and that you'll make an extremely able deputy ... if you choose to exert some of that charm I know you do possess and can employ when it suits you,' Harry Grayson put forward, smoothly insistent.

Marti heaved a disgruntled sigh, then brightened noticeably as a random thought jogged her memory. 'In any case, I can't possibly go. A whole group of us have already booked in to one of the Snowy Mountains ski resorts for next week,' she relayed somewhat triumphantly. 'They've just had their best falls of the season and it's been ages since I've been able to do any skiing.'

'Then as it evidently hasn't been high on your list of priorities until now, there seems little reason why you couldn't put it off for a couple more weeks, does there?'

Although subtly voiced, there was still that adamant quality to the suggestion that had Marti's brief feeling of victorious relief abruptly dissipating. 'But everyone's expecting me to go, and—and the conditions may not be as good later!' she protested.

'On the other hand, there's always the equal chance they may be even better,' her father wasn't averse to pointing out in an increasingly crisp tone. 'While as for your being expected to go, I've no doubt your cancellation will be accepted without any great furore, and that there will be any number of your equally idle, jet-setting friends both available and willing to repeat their visit by accompanying you at some later date. So let's hear no more about the skiing, hmm? I hardly think it's too much to expect you to give up just a few days of your time in order not only to do me a favour, but also to make some small contribution to the enterprises that provide you with your extremely affluent lifestyle, and all its associated benefits that you somehow seem to have come to value above all else.'

Marti's breathing deepened uncontrollably in response to the, as she considered it, unwarranted censure. After all, he had never given so much as a hint that he'd found her chosen way of life unsatisfactory before, and if he hadn't wanted his family to enjoy every possible benefit of wealth, why had he gone to the trouble of making so much money? Besides, she grimaced huffily, if it had been some other function he had wanted her to attend on his behalf she might not have objected so strongly.

But as it was, the idea of having to travel some one and a half thousand miles north to that remote cattle station on the Cape York Peninsula—the Cape itself being the most northerly point of the Australian mainland; the Peninsula the region where her father had been born—and all for the sake of putting in an appearance at some insignificant event she just knew would bore her to tears, was simply too appalling to contemplate.

Her discontented musings came to a sharp halt as she suddenly recalled one particular part of what her father said, and her glance became somewhat suspicious as it settled on his craggy features which were uncharacteristically devoid of the indulgent expression they normally wore when dealing with her, his only child.

'Just what did you mean by a *few* days of my time?' she queried swiftly. 'I thought you said the rodeo only lasted for *two* days.'

'So it does,' he acceded. 'But there's travelling time to be taken into account too, don't forget.' A pause. 'Plus, another couple of matters I wanted attended to.'

'Such as?'—warily.

'Vern Stephens has advised me there's a couple of properties for sale in the vicinity that he thought I might be interested in having a look at with a view to purchasing one, or maybe even both of them.'

Apart from being the owner of Tullagindi station, Vernon Stephens was also a close friend from her father's childhood, Marti knew. In fact, over the years both he and his wife had been no infrequent guests in her home, so that the titles of Uncle and Aunt she had bestowed on them as a small child had remained to the present day. However, that still didn't explain her father's previous remark.

'So?' she therefore prompted with the same watchfulness.

'So since I obviously can't go myself, someone will have to have a close look at both properties on my behalf, make notes concerning relevant details, even take a few photographs perhaps, and ...'

'You mean, you're expecting me to do all that as well?' Marti broke in with an aggrieved gasp. Wasn't it enough that she was having to attend the rodeo?

'Not only do it, but I'm also expecting you to do it well and to the very best of your ability,' she was advised pointedly.

'But I don't know anything about the land!' She had never had the slightest wish to! 'How could I possibly tell good from bad? It all looks the same to me—red or brown dirt, with grass and trees growing on it. While as for noting relevant details, well, I haven't a clue as to what details to note, relevant or otherwise! Come to that,' she hurried on in resentful tones, 'why does it all have to be done right now, anyway? Surely it could wait until you are able to fly up there yourself in another month or so?'

'Except that, even when I am finally allowed out of this damned bed, I do still have other matters requiring my attention, so it would most likely be two or three months before I'm able to get away. By which time neither property might still be on the market.'

Which wouldn't have been any loss at all as far as Marti was concerned, but she doubted it was a prudent comment to make at that juncture.

'In any event, and as you would have discovered if you'd let me finish,' Harry Grayson continued, giving her a speaking look, 'there's another reason—maybe the most important of all, in actual fact—why I want you to attend to such details while you're at Tullagindi.'

'And that is?'

'Because even though, by all accounts, neither property is operating near its full potential—one even lost the majority of its fencing and some of its buildings in a bad fire that went through the place a year or so ago—Vern is still of the opinion they could both be sound propositions with the right manager in charge to make them into viable concerns again. However, before actually committing myself to anything, I've had it in the back of my mind to approach Farrell . . .'

'That's Uncle Vern's eldest son, isn't it?' Marti cut in impulsively once more. 'I can remember meeting Braden, the younger one, on one occasion a long time ago when he was in town, but I don't think I've ever even seen Farrell.'

'I guess that's not so surprising in view of the fact that, like Braden these days, he usually stays with friends of his own when he comes down. As well as the remote likelihood of his calls to see your mother and me ever coinciding with those rare times when you don't happen to be attending some social function or other, or you're out of town altogether,' her father proposed in ironic accents. Then, before she could comment—indignantly, as appeared likely—he went on, 'Nevertheless, to return to what I was saying. I've been toying with the idea of asking Farrell if he would be interested in managing any such property for me, should I decide to go ahead with the purchase. He knows all there is to know about the region and its peculiarities; I know for a fact that there's no one better with stock; he's got a good head on his shoulders; and he knows how to get the best out of his men.'

Which was all very interesting, she supposed, but . . . 'Not that I can see what any of that has to do with me,' she remarked in a rather bored voice.

'You would have, if you hadn't been in such a hurry to display your lack of interest, because I was just coming to that,' he returned pungently, and fixing her with such a disappointed gaze that she regretted having spoken.

It really wasn't that she didn't want to help him at all, it was just that city life with all the attractions and conveniences it encompassed was her sphere, and she objected strongly to being forced to leave them, even if only for a short while. To her mind, a visit to Tullagindi was on a par to being banished to the ends of the earth!

'For although I can always fill in any gaps with follow-up phone calls,' Harry Grayson continued, 'I believe that not only have the properties to be inspected in person in the first place, of course, but that with regard to Farrell especially, the initial approach should also be made face to face.' Halting, he quirked a brow upwards. 'So now you know exactly what it all has to do with you.'

His meaning wasn't lost on Marti and she stared at him aghast. 'You want me to do that too?'

'And keep on the right side of him while you're doing so.'

'But I don't even know him, as I said! Nor would I know how or where to begin!'

'Oh, I'm sure you'll manage to solve that somehow, provided you put your mind to it,' she was informed suavely. 'After all, anyone who can organise down to the last detail a grand ball for upwards of a thousand people, including hiring the required staff, as I've seen you do before now, shouldn't experience any trouble whatsoever in merely sounding out one person for one prospective position, I would have said.'

'That was different,' she said fractiously.

'As this will undoubtedly be as well. And since the majority of your time these days appears to be taken up with finding just that—something different to do . . .' He spread his hands significantly wide.

'Although hardly in the context you're implying!'

'Well, never mind, princess, I doubt you'll suffer any lasting effects from the experience,' her father dismissed her arguments casually, as if the matter was settled. Which, from his standpoint, she vexedly supposed it was. 'And who knows . . .' His lips began to twitch with lightly mocking humour. 'You may even discover just what life *is really* all about while you're there.'

'Except that I don't happen to consider there is life beyond the city limits,' Marti promptly retorted in bittersweet tones as she prepared to take her leave. There seemed little point in prolonging the discussion when it was becoming more and more obvious that no matter how much the idea rankled, and no matter what arguments she put forward to the contrary, her father wasn't going to allow his proposal to be gainsaid, and without causing a family uproar by flatly refusing, there was absolutely nothing she could do about it.

That had been ten days ago, and although Marti might have become resigned to her father's proposal during the intervening period, she was still no more reconciled to it than she had been on first hearing it, so that now, as she stepped from the plane at Cairns in the far north of the Australian State of Queensland, a niggling resentment continued to seethe within her.

She didn't need to see the graceful, waving palms and other lush, colourful vegetation that decorated the airport and its surrounds to know she was now in the tropics. She could feel it, smell it, in the warm flower-scented air that immediately enveloped her, although not even these pleasant sensations were sufficient to relieve her feelings, because they only served to remind her just how far she was from where she wanted to be. As did the now out of place, heavier clothing she had worn in deference to Brisbane's somewhat chillier, late-winter temperatures that she had been experiencing a mere couple of hours previously. Consequently, when she began making her way into the blue-tiled and carpeted terminal along with the rest of her fellow passengers she was in a distinctly less than joyful mood.

She was a tall girl of some five feet six inches, and the classically designed, cinnamon-coloured wool suit she was wearing together with a cream silk blouse, the neckline of which was adorned by a number of both delicate and chunky gold chains, along with the chic high-heeled shoes that set off a length of shapely leg, only seemed to emphasise her height. Although it wasn't just that, or the indisputably affluent picture she presented, that had many a glance turning in her direction.

At twenty-one, she was also possessed of a finely boned, oval-shaped face surrounded by a sleek fall of shoulder-length hair the colour of golden honey with the sun shining on it; darkly fringed green eyes set above high cheek-bones; a slender, slightly retroussé nose; and a generously wide, upward curving mouth. Together with a well proportioned, lissom figure, it was a combination that more often than not brought her a great deal of attention, particularly from the opposite sex, but today she was oblivious to anything of the kind as she literally stalked across to the carousel in order to collect her luggage.

This finally done, Marti stacked the four pieces into a trolley and moved to one side of the hall, her gaze beginning to scan those others present somewhat impatiently. So just where was Uncle Vern's son, Farrell, who she had been informed would be meeting her? He might at least have made an effort to be there on time! Then suddenly her skimming glance came to rest on one particular masculine figure as he strode towards her end of the hall, and because he stood out, not only as a result of his style of dress, but also because a certain look about him made him seem vaguely familiar somehow, she followed his progress with analytical eyes.

She guessed him to be six foot two or thereabouts, and somewhere in his early thirties. A large man, as she was aware a great majority of those born and raised in the bush often were, he was also powerfully built and possessed ruggedly striking features rather than merely good-looking ones. The arms exposed by the rolled sleeves of his drill shirt were corded with muscle and tanned to a shade of teak by years working beneath a scorching sun. As were the long, iron-muscled legs visible below heavy-duty shorts that fitted neatly to lean hips. On his feet he wore short-sided stock boots, thick woollen socks turned over the tops, while on his dark head a broad-brimmed hat rested firmly. Another two marks of the northern grazier, she noted, adding to her surmise that he might well be Farrell Stephens.

Nevertheless, it wasn't until he smiled and returned the greeting of a man passing him that Marti was certain her deduction was correct, because in that split second the resemblance to her Uncle Vern had been unmistakable, and accordingly she began pushing her trolley towards him with determined steps.

Up close, she found he appeared even larger and more muscular than he had from a distance. And more attractive came the unbidden, and unappreciated, assessment as her gaze took in the ebony-lashed hazel eyes, the well-defined nose, and the clean chiselled line of his jaw. His mouth was firm and pleasingly shaped, although becoming etched with a definite trace of irritation as his glance came to rest on her in return. An expression that immediately had Marti wondering what on earth *he* had to look displeased about when it was she who had been kept waiting!

'Farrell Stephens?' she enquired shortly on coming to a halt in front of him.

He nodded, his demeanour not altering one iota. 'While you're Martine Grayson, I presume?'

A brief dip of her own head this time and then she was accusing, 'You're late! My flight arrived almost fifteen minutes ago!'

'Really? he countered on an unimpressed note, and looking as if he couldn't have cared less. 'Then I guess it must have been early, because it wasn't due until only three minutes ago.' He raised a negligent hand to indicate one of the clocks placed about the hall to prove his point.

'Oh!' Marti found herself flushing involuntarily beneath his sardonic regard, much to her surprise. 'I—well ... I'm sorry,' she just managed to force out, grudgingly. She wasn't accustomed to, nor exactly in the mood for, apologising—especially to someone who kept eyeing her in such a deprecatory manner. In an effort to put the incident behind her as quickly as possible she went on swiftly, 'So where's the plane that's to take us to Tullagindi?'

'Who said there was one?'

She pressed her lips together vexedly. Obviously he was being deliberately difficult. 'But Uncle Vern has his own, I know he does, and presumably you fly it too, don't you?'

'When the occasion arises,' he shrugged.

'Well, then?'—with increasing exasperation.

Farrell's mouth firmed no less implicitly. 'We happen to be travelling by road.'

By road! Her widening green eyes reflected her incredulity, and annoyance, at the thought. Too often had she heard her father laughingly decry the state of the roads, or tracks, on the Peninsula for her ever to experience the smallest desire to traverse them. 'But Uncle Vern always flies Daddy to Tullagindi from Cairns when he comes up for the rodeo!'

'Mmm, but then I'm not my father, and you sure as hell aren't yours either, sweetheart!' he drawled with caustic mockery.

Marti sucked in a sharp breath. 'Not that I can see what that has to do with anything!' she snapped. Once again, she didn't know what he had to complain about.

She was the one who had been forced into making the journey!

'Then perhaps this will help explain it,' he returned in equally clipped accents. 'The plane was required at the property, but even if it hadn't been, I can't see any reason why I should put myself out by altering my arrangements to come by road, just for the sake of some pampered and self-centred socialite it wasn't my wish to collect in the first place!'

'Oh!' She stared at him in a mixture of shock and fury. How dared he criticise her in such a manner— even if he had apparently been coerced into the arrangement the same as she had, as would seem to be the case. 'Well, it wasn't my idea that I should come either, I'll have you know!' she retorted.

He uttered a short, satirical half-laugh. 'Since you've never before been bothered to accompany your father on a visit to the area where he was born, do you really think it was necessary for you to tell anyone that?'

'Then maybe I shouldn't have come this time either!' Marti flared, beginning to turn on her heel.

'So why did you?'

She halted, suddenly remembering it wasn't only the rodeo she was supposed to see, and that it was this man her father had wanted her to keep on good terms with! A seemingly unlikely, not to say already begrudged task, in view of their mutual hostility to date. But because she *didn't* want to disappoint her father, despite her reluctance for the undertaking, she now made a valiant effort to subdue both her temper and her feelings of indignation.

'Because, since he wasn't able to come himself, Daddy asked me to take his place,' she replied at length in stiff but cooler tones.

'Asked, or commanded?' came the sardonically astute question.

Marti's chin lifted to a challenging angle. 'Doubtlessly in much the same way as it was evidently suggested that you collect me,' she gibed bittersweetly.

Farrell had no compunction in nodding his agreement. 'At least you understand the position.'

Which didn't augur at all well for the proposition she had to put to him, she deduced with a grimace. Meanwhile, though . . . 'In which case, I'm sure you won't have any objections if I charter a plane to fly me to Tullagindi instead,' she put forward smoothly. 'Is there anyone in particular you can recommend?' Her winged brows arched enquiringly.

'Yes, myself!' he bit out with sudden savagery as, catching hold of her arm in a steely grip, he began hustling her and her trolley out of the terminal unceremoniously. 'Because I'm damned sure I didn't wait around town for an extra couple of days just to have you decide that travelling by road doesn't meet your jaded requirements! Besides,' his firmly moulded mouth took on a mocking curve, 'your father thought you'd be able to see more of the area this way.'

So it had been her own father, via Uncle Vern no doubt, who had arranged that she make such a journey! Oh, how could he have done such a thing when he knew very well she wasn't the slightest bit interested in seeing anything other than what she absolutely had to? If he'd thought to play a joke on her, she failed to find anything remotely amusing in the stratagem. Nor did she take kindly to being manhandled in such an arbitrary fashion either, she fumed, at last trying to pull her arm free from Farrell's grasp.

'All right, all right! So I'll be travelling by road!' she conceded on a flaring but huffy note. It seemed she wasn't to be given any choice. 'You don't have to get all physical about it!'

Relinquishing his hold as they crossed the road that separated the terminal from the parking area, Farrell flexed a wide shoulder indifferently. 'It was starting to appear the only way in which to impress on you that the existing arrangements were going to stand.'

'Well, how was I to know you'd remained longer in Cairns just for the purpose of collecting me?' she defended. 'Moreover, judging from your previous remarks, I would have thought you'd have been only too pleased not to have to take me with you.' Just as she would have enjoyed the absence of his company!

'That's as may be,' he wasn't averse to acceding. 'But I said I'd collect you, and I keep my word.'

More was the pity! Marti grimaced as they came to a stop beside a dusty and obviously well-utilised Land Cruiser.

'Although you're going to have to do something about all of these, of course,' Farrell continued cursorily on opening the back door and loading her luggage inside.

'Meaning?' A frown drew her brows together.

'Meaning, you're going to have cut down on the number of them, for a start,' she was advised in inflexible tones. 'Like, down to one, and preferably of this size.' Indicating the smallest of her suitcases, he swung them effortlessly into the rear of the vehicle. 'I've got a lot to carry, and in the bush clothes come a poor last in the order of priority.'

'But I've only brought the bare minimum with me!' Marti protested immediately. 'I couldn't possibly reduce them by any more. Not and appear at least reasonably well-dressed, that is.' She paused. 'Neither does the vehicle seem exactly over-full, I might add,' she remarked pointedly on surveying the interior of the Cruiser critically. Admittedly, it already held quite an array of equipment such as water containers, bedrolls, spare parts, ropes, a box of cooking and eating utensils, et cetera, but simultaneously, since the back seat had been removed, there still appeared to be more than sufficient space available for her additions. It was, no doubt, just another instance of his being deliberately difficult because he hadn't wanted to be saddled with her presence, she decided.

'Probably because it isn't fully loaded yet,' Farrell answered her last comment first, on a bitingly sardonic note. 'While as for being suitably well-dressed,' the satiric edge in his deep voice became more noticeably pronounced, 'you'll find that up here a person's judged by what they are, not by what they wear. So as I said, a small case with just a couple of changes of clothing should be quite sufficient,' he concluded with unyielding decisiveness.

'That's preposterous!' Marti expostulated, glaring at him balefully. If he imagined she would be succumbing to such an order willingly, he had another think coming. 'I'll have you know I take a certain pride in my appearance, and since I'll be at Tullagindi for something like a week, I can assure you I have no intention of looking less and less presentable as each day passes because of being forced to wear the same clothes continually.'

'So wash them each day,' proposed Farrell laconically as he closed the back of the Cruiser. He fixed her with a goading look, dark brows lifting. 'Or doesn't Miss High Society know how?'

'Yes, I know how!' she fairly grated between

clenched teeth, her green eyes flashing emerald sparks.
'It just so happens that the majority of my clothes
require dry cleaning. They are very definitely never
washed!'

'Then might I suggest you only select those that can
be,' was the unconcerned reply as he pushed the now
empty trolley into a nearby bay set aside for the carts
and then headed for the driver's door. 'You can brush
up on your washing techniques when we camp
tonight.'

'*Camp!*' she promptly echoed on a horrified note
and hurried towards the passenger's side. No one had
mentioned anything about camping! Of course, no one
had mentioned she would be required to make the
journey by road either, she recalled irately. Flinging
open the door, she fixed the man already seated
behind the wheel with a baleful gaze. 'But I was under
the impression I would be staying in Cairns tonight, at
an hotel!'

'Sorry, but since I'm already leaving later than I
wanted to be I decided it would save more time if we
left this afternoon and camped on the way,' he
disclosed quite unapologetically.

Well, good for him! muttered Marti infuriatedly
beneath her breath. Not because she didn't want to say
anything aloud, but mainly because she was suddenly
discovering it was taking all her time and concentration
simply to get into the vehicle.

They were considerably higher from the ground
than a conventional car, particularly the low-slung
Ferraris and Lamborghinis she was more accustomed
to sliding into, and due to her slim-fitting skirt it was
only after a few ungainly efforts that she was at last
able to lever herself up into the seat, a circumstance
that had her cheeks burning with a self-conscious heat,

knowing her attempts to have been subjected to a decidedly ironic scrutiny.

'Why not try using the grab handle next time?' Farrell recommend mockingly, gesturing with his head to the fitting she could now see above the door. 'You'll probably find it easier and quicker.'

Marti drew a deep breath. Naturally he couldn't have told her that beforehand! 'Thank you. *Now* that I know it's there, I will,' she accentuated between gritted teeth.

Then, as the Cruiser was put into motion and they began heading away from the airport, and after she had recovered her composure somewhat, she went on briskly, 'However, to return to this business of only one case . . .'

'I meant what I said, sweetheart!' was the adamant reply.

'But it's ridiculous to expect . . .'

'One case, and that's final!' He slanted her a relentless gaze. 'Because it you're tempted to try otherwise, I'll pack it for you myself, believe me!'

Marti's breathing deepened uncontrollably. 'I wouldn't advise you to try!'

'You reckon you could stop me?' He quirked a wryly taunting brow.

No, she supposed she couldn't, she had little option but to concede, noting once again the muscular size and undoubted strength of him; Not that the knowledge did anything to mollify her nettled feelings of resentment, nonetheless. Being constantly thwarted wasn't something she was familiar with. There was still one other point to be considered, though, and she voiced it sarcastically.

'Then since I'm apparently not to stay in an hotel tonight either, perhaps you'll also be good enough to inform me just where I'm supposed to store the rest of it while I'm away, mastermind.'

A brief, measuring glance, and Farrell hunched a broad shoulder dismissively. 'No worries, spoilt brat,' he returned with equal satire. 'That will all be taken care of.'

Ignoring the disparaging character-analysis, or at least trying to, Marti continued in the same gibing tone, 'You'll consider it no business of mine, I'm sure, but might I be so bold as to ask, by whom?'

'Some friends of mine,' she was informed with another negligent shrug. 'As a matter of fact, it's their home we're heading for now.'

Marti merely nodded, sighing in resignation, and turned her attention to the backdrop of lush green hills that ringed the area as they made their way along tropical shrub and palm-lined streets. She had already, if rancorously, come to the conclusion that it would be an even greater waste of time and effort objecting to the fact that she was expected to camp in the bush, even though the idea appalled her. Good Lord, wasn't it sufficient that she was visiting the region, without getting that close to it! Farrell Stephens had apparently made his decision in that regard, and that was evidently assumed to be the end of it—her wishes notwithstanding, she seethed.

CHAPTER TWO

FARRELL'S friends, Neville and Leah Travers, were a pleasant couple in their mid- to late forties, Marti discovered on meeting them a short time later. Their house, situated high on one of those verdant hillsides behind the city and surrounded by brightly flowering trees and bushes, afforded magnificent views of the orderly fields of waving green sugar-cane that dominated the valley below, as well as an unsurpassed panorama of the coastline, including Green Island way out on the Great Barrier Reef.

'It's very kind of you to agree to store my excess luggage for me,' offered Marti sincerely to Leah as they all sat drinking tea on the verandah that overlooked the view below. In a lot of ways the older woman reminded her of her own mother as she had bustled about making certain everyone was comfortable and had all they required, and she had warmed to her immediately.

'Oh, think nothing of it.' Leah dismissed her gratitude with a smile. 'Harry Grayson's been a good friend of ours for many years now, so anything we can do for any of his family is our pleasure.' She leant forward conspiratorially, blue eyes twinkling. 'Besides, I know what these men are like. Nev's the same whenever we go travelling. Always complaining I take far more than I need.'

'Except I doubt even you would consider four cases a necessity for a period of little more than a week,' put in Farrell on a sardonic note.

'And maybe I wouldn't have either, if anyone had thought to advise me there were likely to be restrictions!' retorted Marti promptly, actually turning her gaze in his direction for the first time since they had sat down—she had been purposely ignoring him until then—and seeing in full now, because he had dropped his hat casually on to the floor beneath his chair, the dark, reasonably short hair that sat close to his confidently held head, and that showed a wayward inclination to curl.

'I'm glad you said "maybe", because the implication I received at the airport was that you couldn't possibly manage without a single one of those items you'd brought with you,' he reminded her derisively. 'At least, not if you wanted to remain the belle of the ball, as it were.'

'That wasn't my intention at all!' Her denial was hotly made. 'I was merely wishing to look presentable! What's so wrong about that?' Emerald eyes challenged hazel stormily.

'Absolutely nothing,' intervened Leah in soothing tones, obviously sensing the tension building between them. She gave a wry chuckle. 'And quite understandable from a woman's point of view, of course.' Then, with a mock glowering glance across the glass-topped cane table they were seated around, 'While you should be ashamed of yourself, Farrell Stephens! You'll have Marti wishing she hadn't come to the north if you're not careful.'

Not unexpectedly perhaps, he uttered an ironic laugh at that, his teeth showing startlingly white against the rich tan of his skin. What was entirely unanticipated, however, at least as far as Marti was concerned, was the inward jolt she felt in response. A distinctly physical sensation that had her breath catching in her throat and that she found more than a little unsettling.

'You mean, more than she does already?' he countered in a mocking drawl.

'Oh?' It may have been Leah who voiced their surprise, but both her and her husband's eyes reflected puzzlement as they now swung to rest on Marti—who cast the man opposite her a fulminating glance before answering. Even if what he said was true, he still had no right relaying her feelings to all and sundry, especially not to this couple who had accepted her into their home with nothing but warmth and friendliness.

'Yes—well—I'm afraid the—er—outback has never held any great attraction for me,' she began with an uncharacteristically self-conscious stammer. 'I'm just a one-hundred-per-cent city girl at heart, I guess. Although I've always liked Cairns, of course,' she hastened to add diplomatically. 'I've been here a number of times in the past, usually on the way to Lizard Island during the marlin season, or just to visit some of the other islands.'

'And it would be a dull world if we all liked exactly the same things,' allowed Leah understandingly.

'Although I'll be surprised if Marti doesn't change her mind once she's been to the Peninsula,' asserted Nev, a statement that Marti very much doubted but refrained from saying so. 'During my trips up there I've known quite a number of people approach the area somewhat off-handedly, and then hate leaving it again.'

'Nev being one of our drivers when, until a couple of years ago, we used to run one of the companies that do regular tourist safari trips to Cape York during the winter season,' explained Leah.

Marti nodded, and feeling obliged at least to feign an interest she had never previously felt, hazarded, 'The summer's too hot for such tours, I suppose?'

'No, too wet!' was the eloquently laughed reply. 'Immediately the first of the rains appear you'll see all the tourists leaving the Peninsula as fast as they can. Not that you can blame them really, because it doesn't take long for not only the rivers but the roads as well, such as they are,' which had an ominous ring to her listener's ears, 'to become totally impassable. Because if you do become marooned, it can be an extremely expensive exercise to get just yourself out again—your vehicle stays!—and that's only if it's known you're there! It's not described by some as "map and machete country" for nothing.' She sent Farrell a wry look. 'Even if that's not how those who live there consider it.'

A corner of his mouth quirked explicitly, although he didn't reply directly, but turned instead to the man beside him to comment, 'Which reminds me, if we're to make Laura by nightfall, I'd better finish the loading.' He began rising to his feet.

'You're right,' agreed Nev with a nod, following his example and also pushing himself out of his chair. 'I'll come with you and give you a hand,' adding for the two women as they began to take their leave, 'We shouldn't be too long.'

'In the meantime I'll pack a picnic lunch for them to eat on the way,' replied Leah. 'Oh, and you'd better remember to put in one of our old bush showers too. I'm sure Marti would prefer that to a bucket.'

Her husband nodded, although Farrell merely raised one hand in an indeterminate gesture that could have been agreement or dismissal as they departed, and leaving Marti to query with a frown, 'Bush shower?'

'Mmm, it's a thick canvas bag with a shower nozzle attached to the bottom of it and a couple of hooks to the top. You simply fill it with water and hang it from any suitable tree or whatever, turn a valve, and you've got your shower,' the older woman explained. 'It's not as good as your one at home, of course, but it's sufficient, and I've certainly always found it preferable to dousing myself by way of a bucket like the men usually do.' This was accompanied by an expressive laugh.

To be truthful, neither method sounded particularly attractive to Marti, but once again she didn't relay her thoughts aloud, commenting, in lieu, 'Oh, but I thought that, with all the rivers I've heard are up there,' despite her lack of interest, at least some of her father's stories on the subject had somehow still managed to find a way into her mind, 'we would be using those for a long leisurely bath.' And that only after learning they would be camping, of course!

'Oh, no!' Leah shook her head decisively, looking aghast at the suggestion. 'Although they can withstand an occasional such use, they can't constant doses because the soap just builds up and eventually kills everything in the water, plus making it unfit for drinking, naturally. Luckily all the tour operators ensure their passengers only use showers or buckets on the banks, and the word gets passed on to all those making individual journeys too, so all the rivers up there are still in their natural, unpolluted state—which is one of the beauties of the region.'

'I see,' Marti nodded, sucking in a disgruntled breath. Oh, lovely! She had the choice of a bucket or a canvas bag for washing! This was going to be even worse than she had imagined! But as she took a sip of her tea a slightly more promising thought came to mind and she mentioned it hopefully. 'Even so, wouldn't the soap consolidate in the ground and eventually still seep into the water?' If it did, there was little reason for not using the river, was there?

Leah's shake of the head dashed her hopes. 'Luckily our wet season prevents that from happening by virtue of the monumentally increased volume of water the rivers carry for those months of the year. As I'm sure your father must have told you, they can rise by anything up to, or even over, sixty feet, which naturally produces an equivalent increase in the rate of flow, and thus they're able to dilute and dispose of any such substances without suffering any ill effects.'

'And flooding everything for miles around while doing so,' added Marti in ironic accents, abruptly recalling more of her father's unprompted information.

'Quite frequently,' was the dry confirmation that brought a rueful smile to Leah's face but only a polite one to her companion's.

How typical of the outback, grimaced Marti to herself. What was it that those who lived in the bush said about it? Oh, yes, that it was a region of permanent drought, relieved only by intermittent floods! Talk about all or nothing! It seemed as good a reason as any for keeping to the city, and simply reinforced her decision always to do just that.

'However, now I guess I had better see about packing that lunch for the two of you,' Leah went on, replacing her cup on the table and beginning to gain her feet. 'While I do, perhaps you'd like to change into something cooler and more suitable for travelling.'

Still dressed in the fashionable winter suit she had

arrived in, even though minus the jacket now, Marti nodded appreciatively. It must have been at least ten degrees warmer in Cairns than it had been in Brisbane when she left earlier that morning. 'As well as reduce the amount of my luggage—as ordered—I suppose,' she said with a sigh as she followed Leah to the spare room where her suitcases were already standing. 'Not that I'm sure just what I'm expected to leave out.'

'Oh, I'd just take one dress, for the dance on the Saturday night of the rodeo, and make do with casual clothes for the rest of the time, if I were you,' supplied Leah helpfully as she turned to leave. 'You know—jeans, slacks, shorts—that sort of thing.'

Marti stared at her incredulously. 'But it's mainly dresses I've brought with me! After all, Daddy did say the rodeo was one of *the* social events of the year up here.'

'Mmm, although not of the kind you were evidently picturing.' Leah eyed her part wryly, part pityingly, the latter an emotion Marti couldn't recall ever having been directed towards her previously. She now found it slightly disconcerting as a result. 'I mean, the Tullagindi Rodeo is no champagne and caviar affair under umbrellas on the lawn of some small-holding on the outskirts of a capital city where people pretend they're in the bush. This is the real thing. It's an event that's run by a committee of local people, with local people taking part, even though these days they do get many competitors coming from further and further afield as more people hear about it. All the same, it's definitely no professional show, and no professionals take part. Just everyday stockmen, real men of the saddle, who like to ride and the challenge of giving it a go.' She paused, her expression kindly as she took in the rather bemused and dismayed look on the younger girl's face. 'You'll also find it hot and extremely dusty—another reason for that casual gear—and if you want to see the action you'll have to perch yourself on the rails just like everyone else. You won't find anything equivalent to a select members' stand up there, I'm afraid. It's a case of everyone rubbing shoulders with everyone else.'

'I see,' murmured Marti pressing her lips together, her resentment at her father's insistence that she come returning in full force. She also had no intention whatever of perching herself on any damned rails!

It all sounded perfectly hellish, not to mention utterly wearisome. Oh, how she wished she were back in Brisbane contemplating a weekend of more agreeable activities: an evening at an exclusive restaurant wining and dining with friends who also enjoyed such pursuits; a day's leisurely sailing on Moreton Bay, where she could anticipate a catered champagne and delicious seafood lunch; or maybe even a party or two. In fact, *anything* that didn't involve setting foot beyond the city's boundaries! She released a disgruntled, helpless breath. If her feelings for not wanting to disappoint her father hadn't been so strong, she would have been tempted to catch the very next plane going south, and to hell with the Tullagindi Rodeo!

With Leah's departure, Marti reluctantly gave her attention to her luggage, changing first into a pair of bottle-green tailored slacks, a delicately printed blouse to which she added a green scarf knotted loosely about her slender neck, and a pair of low-heeled, soft-kid sandals.

It took some considerable time for her to make a final decision as to just which of her remaining apparel she would take with her, but perhaps even longer to force the lid on the now bulging case to close. Farrell Stephens may have considered "a couple of changes of clothes" sufficient, but she certainly didn't! Besides, there were other necessities too—shampoo and hair conditioner, body lotions, facial moisturisers and creams, make-up, all of which she had absolutely no intention of travelling without.

When she at last emerged from the room, doing her best to make it appear that the case she carried weighed far less than it actually did, both the men had apparently returned, and hearing their voices along with Leah's coming from the rear of the house, Marti made her way towards them. She located them in a large, old-fashioned kitchen furnished with polished wooden dressers and copper pots and pans.

Farrell and Neville were seated at a round pine table when she entered, something their host had just said making Farrell smile broadly and, as had happened when she had seen him laugh previously, it generated within Marti a peculiar feeling of awareness in response. She promptly attempted to convince herself it was simply because it displayed an entirely different side to him from the brusque, antagonistic one he seemed to reserve for her. However, as this only engendered the even more disturbing revelation that she could have been beginning to wish it otherwise, she hastily repressed all such unwelcome thoughts and replaced them with a more protective astringency.

'One small case, as commanded,' she quipped acidly on placing it none too gently beside Farrell's chair.

A lazy curve caught at one corner of his mouth, lending his good-looking face a subtly provoking cast. 'It's surprising what you can manage when you try, isn't it?'

'Except that, had I been *allowed*,' she stressed

pointedly, 'to fly to Tullagindi, I wouldn't have been put to the necessity,' she returned dulcetly, refusing to let him get the better of her.

'But just think what you would have missed out on.'

'Oh, I do, I can assure you!'

'An undoubtedly never-to-be-repeated night in the bush,' he began listing mockingly.

'Just as doubtlessly never-to-be-forgotten either!' she shot back pungently.

'Sleeping beneath the stars.'

Marti swallowed, and momentarily her control started to slip as anger made a reappearance in her voice. 'You mean there won't even be a tent?' she glowered. Why, the bush was alive with all manner of things that crept and crawled and slithered!

Farrell hunched a heavily muscled shoulder indifferently, his expression informing her all too clearly that he had no time for the penchant for every comfort. 'Your father always enjoys an occasional night camping and sleeping under the stars. Would we—could we—expect any less of his daughter?' he countered smoothly, although his eyes were shaded with irony.

The louse! Marti smouldered impotently. He knew damned well that where the great outdoors was concerned, she and her father had nothing at all in common! At the same time, though, she still didn't intend him to defeat her that easily and, forcing down her irritation determinedly, managed to return his hardened gaze with a creditable show of unconcern.

'Oh, well, I suppose it saves having to open the window to let some air in,' she proposed whimsically.

'As well as saving time by not having to pitch the tent at night, or pull it down again next morning,' put in Neville on a rueful note of experience.

'Something he hates doing, as you may have surmised by his tone,' interposed Leah with a chuckle as she placed two insulated containers on the table. Her eyes sought Farrell's. 'Well, your lunch is ready whenever you are. Will you have another cup of tea before you go? It won't take me a minute to make a fresh pot.'

With a shake of his dark head, Farrell rose lithely upright. 'No, we'd better not, thanks all the same, Leah. I think it's more than time already for us to hit the road. We've got a lot of miles to cover.' Pausing, he flicked an expressive glance in his passenger's direction. 'And I sincerely doubt Marti would appreciate making camp in complete darkness.'

Marti very definitely *knew* she wouldn't, but since that was the case, she was a little surprised that he hadn't ensured they did just that. When all was said and done, to date he had certainly appeared determined that she should suffer everything she disliked the most.

'Yes, of course,' averred Leah. 'I can't really say I enjoy it myself. It does make everything that much more difficult to accomplish.'

'For me in the main, she means, of course,' contended Neville banteringly as, with Farrell carrying Marti's case and Leah the lunch boxes, they all headed outside.

Stopping at the rear of the Land Cruiser in order to load the three extra items, Farrell eyed Marti mockingly. 'And now you know why I stipulated only one case,' he remarked drily, nodding towards the interior.

Involuntarily, Marti's eyes widened in astonishment. Earlier there had been a reasonable amount of space available, but now there hardly seemed an inch to

spare anywhere. Then she shrugged dismissively.
'Although why it's necessary to carry so much, I've no
idea.' There wouldn't have been any additions made
for the sake of her comfort, of that she was certain.

His mouth tilted in a sardonic gesture. 'Mainly
because, when you live something like four hundred
miles from a recognised shopping centre, you tend to
make the most of it when you do get to town.'

'Oh, well, I wasn't to know that, was I?' she flared,
taking exception to the acid note in his voice.
'Anyway, what about that place where Daddy was
born? What's the name of it? Oh, yes, Coen. That's a
town, isn't it? And I presume it's in the same general
area as Tullagindi.'

'More or less,' he owned ironically, his demeanour
informing her extremely plainly that he was less than
impressed with the vagueness of her knowledge in
view of the number of times her father had revisited
the town of his birth. 'Except that a town with a
population of merely a couple of hundred people, as
welcome as it is to those who live in the district, can
still only be expected to provide the most basic of
necessities. Anything out of the ordinary,' he executed
a philosophical shrug, 'has to be sought further afield.'

Still harbouring ruffled feelings as a result of his
initial reply—now inflamed by his deprecatory look—
Marti took pleasure in using the opportunity to score a
point of her own. 'All of which just confirms my belief
that the city *is* the only place to be,' she fired back
with a taunting smile before making for the front of
the vehicle.

With their farewells to Leah and Neville completed,
they were soon on their way down the hill and leaving
Cairns behind as they headed northwards between
paddock upon paddock of waving sugar-cane.

After a time the canefields were left behind too as they followed the coastal highway where the hills came down almost to the water's edge and the road occupied a small strip between the two. It curved its way closely around each headland and bay, every one of the latter possessing a deserted, palm-fringed, golden-grained beach lapped by a clear, azure sea.

It was quite magnificent scenery and while they passed it Marti was more than content to enjoy it in silence, but as the hour progressed and they began climbing the ranges, heading inland and into the bush that interested her so little, she at last found it necessary to break into speech. Even talking to the impossible man with her would be better than simply sitting there dwelling on just where she was going, she decided.

'I understood from a comment Leah made that this wasn't supposed to be a particularly good road,' she began as the sealed surface they were following wound its way around and over another range of hills.

'Don't rush it,' Farrell advised on a dry note. 'Enjoy what you have, while you've still got it.'

Although Marti scowled at the obviously facetiously voiced suggestion, she was soon wishing she had taken the advice. For very shortly the bitumen did indeed come to a sudden halt, leaving them with an admittedly graded but still rock-endowed road to traverse that not only had them bumping and bouncing in all directions, but also had the Cruiser vibrating with noise so that conversation became decidedly more difficult.

'For how long does this continue?' she had to raise her voice to enquire in long-suffering accents.

'How far are you going?' came the satirical quip.

'You mean, that was the last of the sealed road?' she

asked with a gasp. Heavens above, they'd hardly started their journey!

'Just about, apart from a couple of sections we'll be passing before long,' Farrell replied negligently. 'They generally lay some more each year, doing the worst sections first.'

'This doesn't qualify as one of those?' she countered, sarcasm uppermost. 'And isn't it about time it was regraded, anyway?'

'It was—a couple of months ago,' he disclosed in an aggravating, seemingly amused drawl. 'It won't be done again now until after the next wet season.'

'In other words, you're saying this is what we can expect all the way to Tullagindi,' she said testily.

A corner of Farrell's mouth sloped crookedly. 'Apart from where it deteriorates even further, of course. As Leah implied, the roads on the Peninsula *don't* exactly make for smooth travelling.'

That was the understatement of the year! fumed Marti. 'No, they're more like damned goat-tracks!' she snapped and went back to glaring at rather than surveying the passing scenery for a time.

A surfeit of that was soon reached, however, and chancing to remember something else Leah had said, she eventually returned her gaze to the man beside her, a surprisingly wayward curiosity finally getting the better of her. 'I gather both days during the weekend are taken up with this—er—rodeo, is that right?' she asked casually to begin with.

'Don't tell me you're actually interested?' Farrell slanted her a brief, mocking gaze.

'Never fear!' she promptly gibed right back. 'Nevertheless, since I am having to attend . . .' She both shrugged and grimaced explicitly.

'Mmm, I thought it was too much to expect.'

'Yes, you really should have known better, shouldn't you?' she was only too willing to agree. 'Although you still haven't given me an answer.'

'In that case,' he flexed a drill-covered shoulder dispassionately, 'yes, the rodeo does occupy the whole of the weekend. Although the camp-drafting that takes place on the Saturday isn't strictly a rodeo event, as the ones that are held on the Sunday are.'

'Camp-drafting?' Her brows arched in query.

The look that was bestowed on her this time wasn't merely sardonic, it was thoroughly disparaging as well. 'My God, haven't you been bothered to listen to *anything* Harry's told you about life on a cattle station?' he bit out.

Experiencing an unaccustomed feeling of discomfort at knowing him to be correct, even if she did simultaneously resent the criticism and him for presuming to voice it, Marti elevated her chin with a defensive haughtiness. 'So what makes you so certain he has told me anything about it?' she temporised.

His ebony-framed eyes raked her disdainfully. 'Because, knowing your father and his feelings for this country as well as I do, I'm also aware it would be a sheer impossibility for him not to have done so!'

She swallowed, her gaze dropping a little. 'Well, what if he did, then?' she was reduced to blustering. 'Just because he likes everything connected with the bush doesn't mean I have to listen with bated breath to every word he has to say about it! I've got my own life to lead!'

'Which is totally funded by that very same father, of course!'

'The same as yours is by Uncle Vern,' she sniped immediately.

'Except that mine isn't entirely!' he revealed

trenchantly. 'In any event, I usually put in fourteen to sixteen hours a day for whatever returns I receive.'

'And so am I working for mine at the moment!'

Farrell uttered a contemptuous sound deep in his throat. 'One week out of how many years, twenty-one? Well, how about that?' A biting sarcasm began to surface. 'That's what I really call earning your keep!'

'While I wasn't aware I needed your approval as to how I live my life!' she told him fierily.

'Nor your father's either, apparently, if his disappointment at not having been able to persuade you to forgo your self-absorbed, jet-setting activities *just once* in order to attend the rodeo with him is any gauge!'

'That's not true!' The denial was ground out furiously. There were plenty of home truths she would dearly have enjoyed levelling at him too, if she hadn't been restricted by the fact that she wasn't supposed to alienate him, an assignment that was rapidly appearing farcical! 'It is because I didn't want to disappoint him that I'm here now! Not that he's ever expressed any such feelings to me previously, anyhow.'

'No?' Farrell raised a highly sceptical and satirical brow. 'Well, he certainly has often enough when he's been here. Or maybe, knowing you wouldn't even be bothered to listen—let alone care—he was just too indulgent to voice them as forcefully as he could have!'

About to protest further, his last comment suddenly prompted a string of memories within Marti that had her putting a brake on her words, and biting her lip in momentary indecision as she mentally recounted them: the undisputed tolerance her father had always displayed towards her, and the fact that his face had been uncharacteristically devoid of that benevolence when he had first mentioned his proposal for her to

attend the rodeo in his stead; his inflexible ulti-
matum—so rare where she was concerned—that his
wishes weren't to be gainsaid; and last, though by no
means least, his equally unprecedented and unexpected
contention that it was time she made some contribution
to the enterprises that sustained her chosen lifestyle,
just as the man beside her had more or less implied
only a few minutes ago! It forced her into wondering
for the first time ever if maybe she had selfishly taken
advantage of her parent's lenient attitude. Her
eventual, painfully honest, admission that she probably
had brought a discomfited tinge of colour to her
cheeks as a result.

The flush obviously wasn't missed by her companion. 'Right, was I?' he now surmised goadingly.

'That is a matter which concerns my father and
myself only,' Marti snubbed, refusing to confess
anything to the kind to him. 'I'm here now.'

'Even if under duress,' he inserted relentlessly.

Which, with a supreme effort, she just managed to
ignore. 'Nothing else relating to my family's affairs is
any of your damned business!' she concluded on a taut
note, wondering how she could have permitted him to
sidetrack her to such a degree. All she had done
originally was to make an innocent enquiry regarding
one of the weekend's events.

'Apart from when it involves me too, that is, of
course,' put in Farrell, tight-lipped.

'What do you mean, involves you?' A confused
frown creased Marti's smooth forehead. 'How could it
possibly?'

'Because I'm the one unfortunately having to escort
you to Tullagindi, remember?' He was grimly ironic.
'It's also fallen to me to show you the two properties
Harry's interested in. But if you mistakenly think I'm

going to treat you with the same kid gloves your father obviously does, or that I'll be enduring your peevish tantrums in silence whenever anything isn't to your liking, then I suggest you think again, because it's just not on, sweetheart!'

There had been nothing remotely endearing in the way he'd ground out that last word, but then, neither had she expected there to be. Nor had she anticipated his believing he needed to spell out that there wasn't a single ounce of consideration to be found in his whole rugged body.

'You surprise me,' she quipped tongue-in-cheek on a sweetly caustic note. 'After all, you've shown such unbelievable forbearance, such heart-warming compassion to date, haven't you?' An arched brow peaked meaningfully. Then, in sharpening tones, and without waiting for a reply—if one had been forthcoming— 'Nonetheless, if you also happen to be labouring under the misapprehension that I'm about to jump to attention every time you snap your fingers, or that I'm going to suppress or alter my opinions simply to suit you, then *I* might also suggest you have another think too, *lover*,' the last word was accentuated facetiously, 'because I can assure you that, despite your autocratic and tedious carping, I have absolutely no intention of doing anything of the kind!'

'In other words, once a spoilt brat, always a spoilt brat, eh?'

Marti inhaled deeply, her hand itching to lash out against his lean, deeply bronzed cheek. If he said that just once more! she seethed inwardly. Outwardly she did her utmost to appear unaffected and merely lifted a haughty brow. 'Is that your stock phrase?' she mocked with an exaggerated sigh.

Farrell flexed an indifferent shoulder. 'It would

seem appropriate, don't you think?' He flicked her a goading gaze.

'No, I don't!' she snapped unthinkingly, and could have bitten her tongue for having revealed that he had managed to get under her skin. Her composure recovered slightly, she angled her head higher. 'And nor, might I add, does anyone else I know.'

'Probably because they're as pampered and self-centred as you are,' he didn't hesitate to contend in sardonic accents.

Within their dark frames, Marti's eyes flashed stormily. 'Well, at least they're not obnoxious, overbearing, sermonising pains in the neck!' she flared, giving up all pretence at dissembling and, as much as she was able to, turning her back on him to stare unseeingly through the open window as they continued to bump and jolt their way north.

Behind her came an indistinct sound that could have been a derisive snort or a muffled laugh of disdain, and instinctively she shot a suspicious look over her shoulder, ready to do battle again at the thought of him laughing at her. The fact that she did indeed discover a wryly humorous curve to be playing about his lips succeeded in escalating her feelings of rancour, although only to have them subside a little again when he spoke.

'It would appear you don't exactly object to throwing a few recriminations around yourself, sweetheart,' Farrell drawled lazily.

'It seemed appropriate,' she quoted his own words back at him coolly. 'A dose of your own medicine, you might say. After all, I did tell you I had no intention of suppressing my opinions simply to suit you.'

'It might be advisable if you kept in mind, for future reference, that I also informed you that you

wouldn't be receiving any of the special treatment
you've evidently used to getting either,'—warningly.

Did he really think she needed any reminding?
'Don't worry, I'm sure if I should forget, you'll have
no compunction whatsoever in bringing it to my
attention,' she retorted before returning her glance to
the side.

Much to Marti's relief for the opportunity it
provided to stretch her legs a little, as well as a
temporary respite from the rigours of the road, they
stopped for their lunch at a sandy river in the middle
of the hot, still, and dry bush. Even the watercourse
itself was devoid of water except for a couple of
shallow, brackish-looking pools in its bed, although
the evidence was there in the great tree-trunks that
were strewn haphazardly across it, and the debris still
caught among the branches of those that had survived
the great torrents of water that could, and did, flow
down it when the heavy summer rains arrived.

Within minutes Farrell had a fire going and a billy-
can, filled with water from the container they carried,
stitting over it to boil for their tea. While they waited
Marti wandered along the riverbed for a way, but as it
held little interest for her, she soon returned and
began unpacking the food Leah had prepared for
them.

As she did so, she found her eyes straying in
Farrell's direction on a number of occasions, and
noted that whereas his bushman's attire had made
him stand out at the airport, he now seemed to blend
perfectly with his surroundings. Squatting easily
beside the fire in a typical stockman's stance—sitting
back on one heel, the other leg slightly extended—with
a lighted cigarette between his fingers and his shade-
providing hat pulled down low, he appeared the

epitome of the outback as far as Marti was concerned. Only she couldn't understand why the picture had a strange fascination for her rather than the aversion she would have expected to experience. In an attempt to channel her thoughts towards a less disturbing subject she broke into hurried speech.

'The—er—Palmer River we crossed a short while back,' she began, saying the first thing that came to mind. 'That would be the same river of last-century goldfields fame, I suppose.'

In the act of pouring the tea from the billy into two enamel mugs now, Farrell halted momentarily in order to fix her with a graphically brow-raised glance. 'Don't tell me that you do actually know *something* about the Peninsula?' he taunted.

'Oh, go to hell!' Her still unsettled emotions had her losing control temporarily. 'I did history in school the same as everyone else!' Pausing, she allowed herself the satisfaction of a gibing half-smile. 'You can hardly blame me if the area's sunk into oblivion since that time.'

'But you can be blamed for not having bothered to listen to anything Harry had to say on the subject,' he countered as he finished pouring the tea and handed her a steaming mug. 'Not to worry, though. That's all about to be rectified, anyway, isn't it?' It was his turn to smile now, chafingly.

Was it? 'How do you mean?' She eyed him askance.

'Well, I'm under instructions from your father, aren't I?'

That was the first she had heard of it! 'To do what?' She was more vexed than dubious now.

His expression took on a look of barely concealed humour, with more than a touch of provocation thrown in. 'Why, to see that you do learn something about the region, while also showing you that there is more to life than you've apparently experienced so far, naturally,' he drawled.

That latter phrase rang a dismayingly familiar bell—as she recalled, something similar had been her father's parting remark on her leaving his room that all-too-memorable day—and Marti could have screamed with rage and frustration. How could her normally so very considerate and lenient father not only have suggested anything of the sort, but do so without mentioning it by so much as a word to her as well? She couldn't believe it, but at the same time that comment of Farrell's made it impossible for her to dispute it either. Although just why it should seemingly hold such importance for her parent she had no idea, and yet it evidently did, the partly disgruntled, partly perplexed realisation followed.

'Well, well, lost for words at last, are you?'

The wryly voiced question suddenly penetrated her consciousness and she responded spontaneously, defensively. Anything rather than let him know just how off-balance she did feel, or how the whole idea rankled.

'Not at all,' she demurred, steeling herself to return his dusky-lashed, hazel gaze with a silky half-smile. 'I was merely wondering if perhaps Daddy had over-rated your ability in that regard, and the task was just too much for you, that's all.'

Farrell's glance narrowed slightly, although his mouth still retained its same somewhat lazy tilt. 'Meaning?'

Her own smile became more chaffingly pronounced. 'Well, you do seem to have a penchant for avoiding giving answers to any questions I do happen to ask, don't you?'

'Avoiding?'—watchfully.

'Mmm,' she endorsed in saccharine tones. 'You immediately appear to prefer going off at a tangent in order to give me another lecture in lieu of a reply.' A hint of uncontrollable resentment crept into her tone and she had to clamp down hard on her emotions to regain its former purring quality. 'I mean, I enquire about camp-drafting, and receive a homily about earning my keep. I mention the Palmer River, and am then derided for *knowing* something about the area.' A significant pause. 'I couldn't help but wonder if it was because you simply weren't capable of replying in a more informative fashion.'

'More likely, I just considered it decidedly more suitable!'

'Except that I was under the impression I was supposed to learn more about life on the Peninsula,' which was bad enough in itself, 'not what your opinions are regarding me, or my particular lifestyle!' she concluded triumphantly and, with a dismissive toss of her head, took a mouthful of her tea—inattentively. 'Oh, that's vile!' The involuntary exclamation that promptly ensued completely ruined her previously victorious air, although right at the moment that was the last thing on her mind as she stared in disgust at the black contents of her mug. 'For heaven's sake, couldn't you at least have warned me there was no milk or sugar in it?'

'Sorry, didn't think of it,' Farrell shrugged quite unremorsefully, and complacently downed a mouthful from his own mug. 'After you've lived for a while in a few mustering camps you learn to drink it without.'

Which might have been all very well for the mustering camps, but they didn't happen to be in one at present! 'Well, where is the milk and sugar, then?'

Marti demanded impatiently. He hadn't made any
move to get them as yet, and she couldn't see any sign
of them near the lunch boxes. 'In the Land Cruiser?'

'Uh-uh!' he advised casually as he reached for a
piece of Leah's barbecued chicken. 'I'm not carrying
any.'

'But you must have known!' she began furiously and
then came to an abrupt halt. Of course he would have
known she wouldn't be likely to drink her tea black
and unsweetened! It was just his way of once again
demonstrating his utter disregard for her. Oh, if only
she had the nerve to douse that so very self-assured
form of his with his damned tea, but somehow a
prevailing sense of self-preservation prevented her
from gratifying that longing. There was just too much
about him—the hard set of his shoulders, the forceful
features, the commanding aura of unyielding masculinity he exuded—that proclaimed such an action
would be imprudent in the extreme, and probably the
more so where she was concerned. Instead, she had to
be content with merely tossing the contents of her
mug on to the sand.

'You'll have no objections if I replace it with just
plain water, I trust?' she queried tightly, already
starting to rise from the tree-trunk she had been
sitting on.

'Help yourself,' Farrell allowed impassively, and
without another word she made her way across to the
vehicle.

A few minutes later, with her mug refilled with
water, more pleasing to her taste if somewhat warm,
Marti didn't immediately return to the fire but
remained where she was, leaning moodily against the
front of the Cruiser, her thoughts introspective, her
spirits somewhat deflated.

Usually greeted warmly wherever she went, her company eagerly sought, it was the first time in her life she had experienced such open contempt for both her mode of living and herself, and she was beginning to find it oddly hurtful. Not that she cared whether Farrell Stephens liked her or not, of course. After all, she would consider herself fortunate if she never saw him again once this visit was over. Simultaneously, though, she would have been lying to herself if she hadn't admitted that his constant censures were beginning to tell on her, or that they had provoked certain feelings of guilt and regret within her when they made her recall just how thoughtlessly she had as good as flaunted her lack of interest in her father's beloved Peninsula.

Suddenly, she realised Farrell was beside her, proffering one of the lunch boxes. 'Here, you haven't had anything to eat yet,' he said.

'I'm not hungry,' Marti sighed, shaking her head.

'You will be before we reach where we're to camp,' he stated on a faintly exasperated note. 'So stop being so childish, and eat something. If Leah was thoughtful enough to provide it, the least you can do is to eat some.'

He had a point there, she supposed, and reached for a piece of chicken acquiescently.

However, before she could raise it to her mouth, a strong brown hand abruptly spanned her chin and tilted her pensive face upwards. 'And for your information, the omission of milk and sugar wasn't deliberate, if that's what you're thinking,' Farrell informed her with a rueful twist to his lips. 'It was purely from force of habit.'

Trying desperately to cloak the ridiculous feeling of pleased relief that flowed through her at knowing it hadn't been done solely to add to her discomfort, Marti looked away swiftly. 'You don't have to explain your actions to me,' she said hopefully on an uncaring note.

'I'm well aware of that,' came the categorical retort as he dropped his hand to rest on a lean hip. 'But I also figured we appear to have enough scope for argument as it is, without the need for any erroneous reasons.'

Marti nodded. He sure wasn't wrong there! she grimaced.

CHAPTER THREE

WITHIN a short while they were on the road once more, although now the increasing heat that had been assailing them ever since they had crossed the ranges that separated the inland from the coast made the journey even less bearable as far as Marti was concerned. Then there was the dust to contend with too. Her clothes were progressively becoming covered with it, her hair felt odiously thick with it, even her skin was developing a noticeable red tinge. But it was just impossible to avoid, she discovered to her disgust, for it was of such a fine texture that it billowed up in great clouds both around and behind the Cruiser, and not even closing the windows when they passed another vehicle travelling in the opposite direction could prevent it from finding its insidious way inside.

'So is this the old goldfields area, then?' she asked somewhat wearily at length, becoming tired of watching the red slash of road they were following through the seemingly uninhabited, never-ending bush.

This time Farrell nodded in answer to the question, not taking his eyes from the road. 'Mmm, not that there's much left to give any indication of just how rich a field it was. Just a few bricks, bottles, and some rusty pieces of machinery dotted about the bush. There's not a building left to show where any of the towns that sprang up stood. Even Maytown, which boasted a population of some ten thousand in its heyday, has disappeared now, except for the solid stone kerbing of the streets that today lead nowhere.'

'I see,' Marti acknowledged in detached tones. Actually, she was inclined to think all those people had done their descendants a favour by leaving such an isolated wilderness, but forbore to say as much. She was just thankful that her own father was one of those who had also departed the Peninsula. 'And camp-drafting? You never did say what that entails exactly,' she went on in much the same dispassionate manner, although she supposed even seeking answers that didn't particularly interest her was an improvement on just watching the scenery go past.

'Oh, it's more or less just a derivation of the practice of drafting out on horseback particular animals from the herd in mustering camps, that's all,' he shrugged in reply. 'Only in competition, once the drafting's been completed, the animal then has to be made to perform a figure of eight around two markers, pass through a sapling gate, and all within forty-five seconds.'

She digested the information meditatively. 'It doesn't sound especially difficult.'

'Except that the steer usually has other, very definite, ideas about where it wants to go,' he drawled wryly.

'Oh!' That hadn't occurred to her. Pausing, her own thoughts now took a rather whimsical turn at it having taken so long for her to get around to the question her curiosity had urged her to ask some hours—and arguments—before. 'And do you also take part in this camp-drafting, and the other rodeo events?'

'Usually in the former,' he confirmed casually. 'Although normally only in the role of pick-up man, or hazer or something similar, with regard to the latter these days, now that I'm older and wiser.' An expressive smile formed about the edges of his shapely mouth.

'Pick-up man, hazer?' Marti repeated bewilderedly. He might just as well have been speaking another language.

Farrell didn't immediately explain. He just pressed his lips together—in despair or exasperation, she couldn't quite decide. 'A pick-up man takes the rider from the bull or horse after his allotted time has expired. The hazer's job is to keep the animal running straight in steer-wrestling and calf-roping events,' he supplied concisely.

She nodded, and thought it perhaps prudent to move on to safer ground. 'So—umm—what made you decide to hold a rodeo at Tullagindi each year, anyway?'

'We didn't originally.' The disclosure was made on an ironic note. 'It began just as a bit of fun for our own hands once the final muster of the year was completed. Then before we knew it ringers from neighbouring stations were joining in and over the years it's just grown from there. Only with so many taking part now we've had to move it to earlier in the season when it's cooler.' A statement that had Marti's eyes widening eloquently. If this was cool, she shuddered to think what hot might be like! 'Also, it's now used as a means for collecting proceeds for charity—the Royal Flying Doctor Service, in this instance—and quite successfully too, we're pleased to be able to say, since for every dollar we raise on behalf of the R.F.D.S. the government contributes another dollar-fifty.'

At last he'd mentioned something Marti could actually associate with, for her mother, and herself to a lesser degree, had been involved with charitable

organisations in Brisbane for many years. Her mother,
especially, was always attending committees and
arranging functions in order to collect funds for a
variety of deserving causes.

'All the same you'd still require quite a sizable
attendance in order to make a really good profit,
wouldn't you?'

'Around here, we consider between maybe three and
five hundred to be a sizable attendance, and we're not
exactly complaining about the profits either,' he
answered drily.

'*That* many attend!' she gasped. She'd had no idea.
'And they come by *this* road?'

'The majority do. Some from as far away as five and
six hundred miles or so. Others, spectators mainly,
arrive by plane, though.'

Precisely as she would have preferred to have done!
While as for those who voluntarily travelled the road
she was on, well, they would have to be unbelievably
keen or else totally out of their minds, she determined
sardonically, her gaze returning briefly to the scene
outside the vehicle.

As they moved ever northwards, Marti was
surprised to notice the scenery beginning to change
about them. In fact, it didn't resemble in the slightest
the outback she had been anticipating at all—flat
plains that seemed to stretch forever, stunted
vegetation, a total lack of landmarks—and actually she
was starting to find it nowhere near as uninviting as
she had initially, although she had no intention of
conceding as much to the man beside her.

For here the landscape would sometimes open out
to show wide, seemingly untouched, tree-covered
panoramas that swept away to the horizon, or give
totally unexpected vistas of broad acres cleared and

under cultivation, and then at other times close in about them so densely that it was impossible to see anything beyond the next hundred yards or so of twisting, hilly road. That was the only thing that didn't alter. It remained as dusty, corrugated, and pot-holed as ever.

A sign, warning of the likelihood of dangerous crocodiles in all lagoons and waterways north of that point, had her swallowing apprehensively at its import, however, and presuming aggrievedly that that was just one more thing no one had considered it necessary to tell her about.

Nor were her feelings of discontent assuaged at all when, late in the afternoon, and after crossing yet another massive, dry bed of a river, they eventually reached the tiny township of Laura, but instead of stopping Farrell continued right past it.

'But I thought you said we'd be stopping the night at Laura!' she rounded on him accusingly.

'A figure of speech only,' he discounted indifferently. 'Our camping spot's on a river a few miles ahead.'

'Well, we could have stopped for a drink at least, couldn't we?' True, there hadn't appeared to be much there beyond a small general store and an old hotel built of corrugated iron with tree-trunks for supports and tin shutters for windows, which looked as if it had been erected to serve the goldminers of the previous century—which it had—but at least it would have provided *some* relief from the heat and dust and continual bouncing.

'There didn't seem much point when we'll be stopping altogether shortly,' Farrell shrugged. 'Besides, if we waste too much time we'll not only be making camp in the dark, but washing in it too.'

'And why would we have to do that?' demanded Marti. 'You've surely got a lamp, haven't you?'

'Uh-uh! Just a torch.' The information was relayed with careless impassivity.

'Oh, marvellous!' She executed a sarcastic grimace. 'You mean, that's all there is to do after dinner? Either go to bed or sit around a blasted camp fire!'

Farrell angled her a satiric gaze. 'So what did you expect, to watch television?'

Her return look was rancorous as she slumped back in her seat. 'God knows, but it wasn't this! Next, I suppose you'll be saying we'll be having a sing-song round it too!'

'If that's what rows your boat,' he agreed facetiously.

Pressing her lips together, she glared at him balefully. She felt hot, tired, and dirtier than she could ever remember, and when there wasn't even the comfort of decent facilities to look forward to, she wasn't in any mood to hide her simmering feelings.

For another hour they lurched and shuddered onwards, dodging some holes and jolting across others that were invisible due to their having been filled with the thick, ever-present bulldust. Finally, though, after crossing even more dry creeks and rivers, they turned off the road, to follow instead a narrow track that wound around stands of tall trees until they came to a large clearing streaked with long shadows to denote the lateness of the hour.

'Well, thank heavens for that!' Marti groaned immediately they pulled to a halt, and hurriedly alighted. 'I feel as if I've been shaken to pieces! That's not a road, it's a cart track!'

'So you implied earlier,' recalled Farrell flatly as he opened the tailgate and began extracting the camping equipment. 'But unloading this gear should help you unwind. Here!' He unexpectedly tossed one of the two swags he was holding towards her, which she caught mechanically. 'You can start by stacking these next to that tree over there.'

'*Me?*' She stared down at the rolled bedding and then back at him incredulously.

'Yes, *you!*' As if to prove his point the second one now followed, only this time she didn't even make an attempt to catch it but allowed it to fall to the ground in front of her. 'I'm not your damned servant, sweetheart, so don't make the mistake of thinking I am!'

'And I'm certainly not yours either!' she flared, now dropping the one she had caught as well. 'So you can get lost, Farrell Stephens! The only thing I'm interested in is having a wash!' She turned on her heel to begin storming away to where she could hear the tinkling sound of running water.

Relentless fingers gripping her arm in a vice-like hold and spinning her back again prevented her from getting very far, however. 'Washing waits until the work's finished, you petulant, uncooperative little bitch!' Farrell lashed at her scathingly. 'So don't come your supercilious socialite act with me, because I just don't intend to put up with it! In camp, everyone does their fair share, and that includes *you*! So now I recommend you go and pick those up,' stabbing a finger towards the two swags, 'and stack them exactly where I suggested without wasting any more time, because you've also got the firewood to collect before you get around to starting even to *think* about washing! Understand?' He gave her a none-too-gentle shake in emphasis.

Momentarily, Marti could only stare at him

speechlessly, her breasts rising and falling rapidly with
her deepened breathing, her temper at boiling-point.
'What I understand is that it's obviously long overdue
for someone to tell you precisely where to get off too,
you—you arrogant, insufferable, boorish cow-cocky!'
she denounced as derogatorily as possible. 'How dare
you talk to me in such a fashion!' Certainly no one ever
had in her life before. 'Who appointed you judge and
jury, anyway? I'm not answerable to you for anything,
anything, do you hear! And take your hand off me too!'
She hit out at him infuriatedly, but although he did
deign to release her, she suspected her hand came off
worse from the encounter than his arm had, because her
fingers now smarted as much from their connection with
his incredibly hard, muscled flesh as her emotions had
from his words. 'Just remember, you were the one who
insisted I come by road!'

'And having got all that out of your system, *now* are
you going to get to work? It's not getting any lighter,
you know.' His eyes turned skywards significantly.

The heavily sardonic timbre in his voice grated
unbearably along Marti's nerves. 'No, I'm not!' she
defied impetuously as a result. 'And what's more, on
similar lines as the proverbial horse being led to water,
I very much doubt you can make me!' A somewhat
taunting light made an appearance within her long-
lashed emerald eyes.

In response, a muscle corded beneath Farrell's sun-
darkened cheeks and a considering glitter entered his
own gaze. 'There are ways and means, Marti,' he
warned in quiet but hard-edged tones.

She swallowed nervously, her heart beginning to
thump to an erratic tempo, but still her pride wouldn't
let her back down so quickly, even in the face of the
perturbingly ruthless look that abruptly seemed to

have settled on his strong-boned features. 'Such as?' she therefore dared to challenge, if a trifle throatily.

'Somehow I suspect you'd regret finding out.'

To be honest, so did she, although she still couldn't bring herself to surrender without at least retaliating in some way. 'You're probably right,' she acceded with doubtful docility. 'After all, it's more than evident you have none of the instincts of a gentleman to guide you, isn't it?' She favoured him with a sweetly gibing smile as she brushed past him.

'Perhaps it's just as well, because you don't precisely embody all that's ladylike either, sweetheart,' the mocking retort followed her.

'In view of the company I'm being forced to keep, that's hardly surprising!' she turned to snipe over her shoulder.

'Mmm, I know the feeling!'

This time Marti didn't condescend to reply, but continued on her way with her head held high to snatch up the swags and then proceed to dump rather than place them beside the appropriate tree.

'Oh, and by the way,' Farrell added in dry tones as he came abreast of her carrying more gear, 'strictly speaking, a cow-cocky's a dairy farmer. I'm not.' He gave a brief tug on the brim of his hat, his lips twitching provokingly as he started back to the vehicle again. 'Just thought I'd set the record straight, as it were.'

Marti stared at his departing back balefully, annoyed with her own ignorance for having provided him with yet another opportunity to discomfit her, and even more infuriated with him for having no hesitation in doing so. With a vexed compression of her lips, she swung about and went looking, cautiously and with no enthusiasm whatsoever, for firewood.

Due to an innate, and ungovernable, dislike for anything that crept or crawled, it made the task a somewhat protracted one as she jumped nervously at every rustle among the dead leaves littering the ground—imagining all manner of poisonous snakes or blustering lizards to be on the move—and gingerly turned over each twig and small branch with her sandalled foot in order to inspect it thoroughly for any insects that might be lurking thereabouts before committing herself to actually picking them up.

'For crying out loud, are you trying to turn it into a lifetime's work?' demanded Farrell impatiently on her return with her second small bundle. 'We need wood as well as damned twigs, you know! That lot won't last any time.' His expression assumed a disparaging look. 'Or are you just hoping that if you take long enough to collect so little, I'll get tired of waiting and end up doing it myself?'

'No, that wasn't it at all!' Marti denied on a rising note, although the idea did have a distinct appeal, naturally. 'I was doing my best! I've just never done anything like this before, that's all!' Not for anything did she mean to reveal the real reason for her dilatoriness. That would merely give him just one more chance to mock her, and the last episode was still too fresh in her mind for that.

'That's obvious!' he endorsed succinctly. 'But might I ask just what's wrong with that branch right there?' Indicating one particular, many-limbed piece of wood not far distant.

'It looked too difficult to drag over here,' she shrugged.

'You couldn't have tried breaking it into smaller pieces, of course!'

'I thought it was too thick.' She was careful not to

mention she had seen a number of small spiders' nests on it also.

Farrell fixed her with a speaking glance and, taking the few steps necessary to reach it, proceeded to snap it into smaller pieces almost one-handed. 'It's from a paperbark, sweetheart. An eight-year-old could break it with equal ease,' he drawled expressively.

'Oh, well, I didn't know that, did I?' she parried with a sinking feeling. Now she supposed he'd expect her to do the same—spiders, or whatever, regardless.

'If you'd made the effort, you might just possibly have found out, though.' He stretched, flexing wide shoulders, and continued in casual accents. 'Anyway, I'll leave you to it. Since there's not enough wood there yet to light a decent fire,' eyeing her meagre pile sardonically, 'I guess I may as well get down to the river for my wash while I'm waiting, and before the light goes altogether.' He cast a meaningful look skywards before bending to retrieve a nylon sports bag, together with a couple of plastic buckets, and then started for the thicker line of trees just behind them.

'And what about me?' Marti promptly shouted after him in furious indignation. 'Or aren't I to be given the opportunity to wash while there's still light available?'

'That all depends on how long it takes you to finish collecting the wood, I suppose,' he called back negligently. 'As I told you before, you wash *after* the work's done.'

If Marti had known how to set up the bush shower that Leah had mentioned, or even where it was, she would have had her own wash there and then, and be damned to Farrell Stephens and his dictates! But as it was, there seemed little she could do to thwart him, and she felt like kicking something in frustration. She had just known this trip was going to be purgatory, and she had never been more right in her life.

By the time Farrell returned some twenty minutes later, dressed in clean shirt and shorts, and not only looking so much cleaner and refreshed but evidently feeling it too—much to Marti's resentment since it only made her feel, and no doubt appear, that much more tired and dirty in comparison—she had, nevertheless, collected considerably more wood, if with the greatest of reluctance.

'*Now* do you think I might possibly be allowed to rid myself of all this wretched dust as well?' she immediately fired at him caustically.

He hunched an indeterminate shoulder. 'Unless you'd rather peel the potatoes beforehand.'

Marti's temper rose uncontrollably. 'No, I don't want to peel the potatoes beforehand!' she seethed. And nor did she intend to do them afterwards, if it came to that! She wasn't the cook for this unbearable trek! 'I just want my shower!' Abruptly, she half-turned away, her shoulders slumping as the full force of her weariness seemed to catch up with her, making any sustained anger impossible. 'As if you didn't know,' she concluded on a dull, dispirited note.

'Mmm, I guess that was rather bloody-minded, wasn't it?' Farrell suddenly allowed gruffly, much to her amazement. And she was even more astonished when she felt his hand come to rest on the nape of her neck, his thumb beginning to move against her soft skin in an unexpectedly soothing fashion. 'It's been a long day for you, hasn't it?'

Becoming all too conscious of the sure and persuasive touch that was radiating warmth downwards from her neck, and concerned by the fact that she was finding herself quite content to have it continue, Marti swallowed and merely nodded jerkily as she pulled away from the disturbing contact.

'Okay, then, I'll fill the shower for you. I brought the water back with me.' He began sorting through a box that he'd set beside the tree and brought forth a rectangular canvas bag and a funnel. 'So where do you want it hung when it's ready?'

She waved a hand somewhat flusteredly, her senses still disconcerted by the effect of his strangely stimulating touch. 'Oh, any—anywhere will do,' she stammered.

'Anywhere?' His expression was wry as he looked around the open clearing.

Marti felt her cheeks flush warmly, betraying her loss of composure, and berated herself unmercifully. Lord, just how adolescent was she to have seemingly lost all control as a result of one brief moment's lack of antagonism? She must be even more tired than she realised, she decided.

'I meant, anywhere suitable, naturally,' she amended as primly as possible.

The slope to Farrell's mouth became slightly more pronounced temporarily, and then it was gone as his manner took a more practical turn. 'In that case, I suppose it had better be within the trees by the river. So go and collect whatever you need, and I'll meet you over there.' With the now filled bag in one hand and another still-full bucket in the other, he started for the area in question, suggesting as he began walking, 'Oh, and you'd better get the torch from the Cruiser too. It'll probably be dark by the time you've finished.'

Only too anxious, and thankful, to do as instructed on this occasion, Marti snatched hold of her bag and the torch and hurried after him, relieved once again at Leah having thought to provide her with a towel since she, not surprisingly, hadn't thought it necessary to pack one herself when she'd left Brisbane.

On reaching the trees that lined the river she found Farrell had already hung the shower from a suitably low branch, but momentarily her gaze was drawn to the scene below them where crystal-clear water rushed and bubbled over a series of smooth rocks, while the last rays of the descending sun burnished the sparkling water with a bronze tinge between the shadows created by the trees.

'Oh, that's pretty!' she exclaimed spontaneously.

'You mean you've actually found something in the bush that appeals to you?' drawled Farrell in the driest of tones. 'I thought only concrete canyons found favour in your eyes.' He began taking his leave.

Marti let him go without answering. Truthfully, she was more than a little surprised herself at experiencing some appreciation for the area. Not that she was interested in analysing the reasons therefore—after all, her return to the city couldn't come quickly enough as far as she was concerned—and dismissing the incidents from her mind nonchalantly, she set about making the most of her long-awaited shower.

Even as basic as it was Marti couldn't remember when she had enjoyed one more. Just to feel all that dust being washed away, especially out of her hair, was divine, and despite having to use the torch once the sun eventually sank below the horizon, she still couldn't resist re-filling the shower an extra time from the river, it was so incredibly refreshing.

Of course, once dried and clad again in a gathered cotton skirt and a matching primrose-coloured blouse, the simple design of which belied its extravagant cost, she found it noticeably less enjoyable as she attempted to follow her normal beauty routine with regard to her face and hair. In the end she had to make do with just a light moisturiser for one, and a rough towelling and combing for the other. Of course, it would have been different if she had been allowed to bring her blow-dryer with her, but no, that had had to be left in Cairns, she recalled irritably, and quite forgetting that without electricity it would have been of no use to her, anyway.

'You were gone so long I thought the swamp dogs must have got you,' Farrell greeted her lazily on her return to the fire which was now burning brightly. The billy, a saucepan, and a couple of appetite-teasing steaks rested on a heavy metal plate above it.

Swamp dogs, Marti repeated to herself with a frown as she seated herself at one end of the large log he'd pulled near to the fire, although only after perusing it carefully. 'Do you mean dingoes?' she queried. Actually, they had seen one padding silently through the undergrowth earlier in the day.

'No, crocs.'

'Crocodiles!' she gulped, suddenly remembering the sign advising of their presence. Until then, it had completely slipped her mind. And to think she had been blithely showering within a few feet of the river. She sent him an extremely graphic, sideways glance. 'Well, thanks for warning me! Or were you hoping they'd relieve you of my distasteful company?'

His firmly moulded mouth shaped indolently. 'Not much chance of that around here,' he took her aback a little by then declaring. His eyes met and held hers meaningfully. 'I just figured that, since you evidently weren't giving them so much as a thought, someone should bring the point home to you, because next time you could be in an area where they are around.'

'You mean, you frightened me half to death by way

of a reminder?' she bristled. 'Oh, that was considerate of you!' She paused, continuing to glower at him. 'In any event, surely I'm entitled to expect you to warn me if there's any likelihood of danger. You're the one who knows the region, not me. Halting again, she hunched a slender shoulder dismissively. 'Besides, no such circumstances are likely to arise once I reach Tullagindi, and since this is the only night we'll be camping . . .' She shrugged implicitly once more.

'Is it?' he countered, much to her surprise, his expression so wry that she swallowed convulsively.

'Well, isn't it?' she demanded on an anxious note. He had said they'd reach Tullagindi tomorrow, hadn't he?

'Not if you intend viewing those properties your father's interested in,' was the bland reply.

Good grief, she'd temporarily forgotten all about them. 'But—but . . .' she spluttered.

'So you see, you,' with an accentuating tap beneath her chin, 'may also be required to keep an eye out for crocodiles, after all,' Farrell asserted in expressive accents.

At last Marti managed to find her voice—her indignant voice. 'But I was under the impression we would be flying to each of them!'

'I don't know why,' he rebuffed, irony predominant. 'Although an aerial view can be quite illuminating, it's still the ground inspection that matters most, and when there's something like two thousand square miles to cover between the pair of them, I, for one, would prefer to do it with a set of wheels under me rather than fly in and then attempt to do it on foot or horseback.'

'Oh!' She pulled a defeated, disgruntled face. Once

again, no one had thought to inform her of that. Nonetheless, now that she had been reminded of the second reason for her journey, she supposed she might as well venture a little further on the subject. 'And— umm—these properties,' she began distinctly less than confidently, unsure if she could recall all the pertinent details her father wanted to know about, and even less certain she had the ability to discover such information without making a complete fool of herself, and a total botch of the whole undertaking. 'I gather Uncle Vern considers them to have—er—some promise, is that right?'

'Uh-huh!' Farrell nodded, leaving the log and sinking into his typical squatting position as he began removing their food from the fire and placing it on a pair of enamel plates. 'Provided the manager employed knows what he's about, of course.' Turning slightly, he handed one of the plates to her, the firelight reflecting a hint of amusement in the depths of his surprisingly long-lashed, hazel eyes. 'That is, if he isn't tempted to return to the Peninsula in order to run it himself.'

It was the perfect opening for Marti to advise him just who her father was anxious to have control over any such contemplated purchase, but at the same time she considered it could perhaps be too soon for that to be mentioned, and so shook her head in negation and declared instead, 'Oh, I doubt that very much, even if the idea did appeal.' Which she strongly suspected it very much would! 'It would be quite impossible for him to run all his other business interests from way up here.'

'Much to your relief, no doubt?'

'How did you guess?'

'Hmm.' His lips levelled explicitly, and then he

caught her off-guard a little by abruptly changing the subject completely. 'So how's the dinner?'

'Oh—er—very nice, thank you—and very welcome,' she owned, recovering. He certainly hadn't been wrong when he'd claimed she would be hungry by the time they made camp. Then, finding it impossible to resist, she added dulcetly, 'Especially the potatoes.'

'I reckoned I might as well get on with it, since it was more than likely you wouldn't know what to do with them, anyway,' came the swiftly mocking retort.

'Oh, I don't know about that,' Marti disclaimed in something of a purr. 'When all's said and done, you do present quite a reasonable—not to say, tempting— target.'

'Quite possibly,' he allowed, although so smoothly that she was instantly dubious. 'But then, just think how infuriating—not to say, mortifying,' he mimicked her own phrasing, 'it would be for you picking them all up again afterwards, if you were ever misguided enough to resort to such an imprudent manoeuvre.'

Yes, retaliation undoubtedly would be both rapid and demoralising, suspected Marti with a grimace, her bantering mood fast dissolving. 'Oh, don't let it worry you. I was only joking,' she flared.

'I wasn't.'

'No, why would you? It's been glaringly obvious ever since I arrived that it's your intention to make every possible aspect of my visit even more dis-agreeable and unpleasant than ...!' Suddenly she broke off, uttering an involuntary cry of alarm and revulsion on catching sight out of the corner of her eye of something quite large crawling across her skirt. Leaping to her feet, she flapped the folds of material frantically in an effort to dislodge it.

'What in hell?' Farrell ejaculated, disposing of his

plate and rising to his feet, although in his case in a markedly less agitated manner.

'There was something pale and horrible crawling on me!' she wailed, unable to repress a series of shudders. 'Oh, God, I wish I'd never come! I hate camping! I hate the bush—and all its horrible occupants! And I hate you too, Farrell Stephens!' Unbidden tears washed into her eyes, but weren't permitted to be shed, not in front of this man.

'Yeah, no doubt,' he granted in rough-edged tones, relieving her of the plate she found, to her astonishment, she was still clutching and depositing it near his own on the log, before bending still further and retrieving something from the ground. 'But for heaven's sake, it was only a harmless gecko!' He opened his fingers sufficiently to show her the sandy-skinned lizard about four inches long that squirmed within, the round adhesive pads on each tiny toe fastening to his skin.

'Oh!' Relieved, but feeling a little foolish, she still faced him defiantly. 'Well, I didn't know what it was, did I? And—and in any case, the thing that was on my skirt was much paler than that.'

'Only because it was trying to tone in with the colour of the material, the same as it's now attempting to do with the skin of my hand,' she was informed on an ironic note. 'If you put it in that tree over there it would soon start to look green, and if you put it on the ground it will go brown.'

'Really?' she suddenly found herself asking in response to a surprisingly piqued curiosity. Why should she care if it turned bright red, even? It belonged to the bush, and that should have been enough to dispel any interest on her part.

'Uh-huh!' Farrell confirmed lazily. 'And, I might

add, it's three times as terrified as you were a moment ago.'

'I was not terrified!' she said immediately, albeit with a somewhat self-conscious flush warming her cheeks. 'Besides, it could have been anything.'

'And because you're so ready to dislike everything about the bush, you naturally just had to assume the worst, hmm?'

Marti shrugged defensively. 'It's not my fault if it's filled with things that creep and crawl!'

'Most of which you would find not nearly so frightening if you bothered to become better acquainted with them. And even you must have grown up playing with lizards of one kind or another. Every kid in this country does, no matter where they live.'

She made an expressive moue. 'Then I must have been the exception, because I didn't.'

Farrell shook his head in disbelief. 'Then now's your chance to remedy that omission, isn't it?' He held out the hand containing the gecko. 'Here! Do you want it?'

About to answer very much in the negative, some unknown reason suddenly had her changing her mind and tentatively reaching out with her own hand even as she queried doubtfully, 'They don't bite, do they?'

'Not unless you hold them too tightly,' he advised as he dropped the surprisingly solid little body into her cupped fingers. 'They don't like to feel pinned down.'

Marti nodded, experiencing a totally unexpected sense of pleasure on feeling those tiny pads clinging to her fingers for security. 'Actually, it's rather cute, isn't it?' She looked up to smile instinctively.

For a time Farrell was silent, his attention appearing to be concentrated on the wide, upward curve of her soft lips. 'You should smile more often. It has a lovely effect on your eyes, and does even nicer things to your mouth,' he declared quite irrelevantly, and then turned away abruptly, irritably almost. 'Yes, well, perhaps you'd better let it go now, anyway, otherwise your dinner is going to be stone cold.'

'I—I guess so,' she faltered, her smile fading quickly, but still making an effort to keep her tone light in order to conceal her own confused, and confusing, reaction to the incident. For one brief, warming moment she had felt as if he didn't disapprove of her entirely, and then he had deliberately dispelled it—and she didn't know why she cared. 'In any event, I think it must be as frightened as you said, because I can feel its poor heart pounding away like mad,' she continued in the same forced manner as she set the little creature to the ground and watched it scuttle to safety beneath some dead leaves.

'And yours?' he queried as he began eating again, his voice sounding sardonically harsh to Marti's ears.

Resuming her own seat, she stiffened apprehensively. 'How do you mean?' He couldn't possibly have realised the disquieting effect his words had had on her, could he?

'Wasn't yours also thumping quite rapidly when you first discovered our visitor?' There was no doubting the satiric inflection now. It was quite pronounced and biting.

'Most likely!' In turn, her own tone became decidedly less restrained as relief coursed through her.

'Mmm, you've still got a hell of a lot to learn about life outside the city, haven't you, sweetheart?'

'Although only if one considers it *worth* learning!'

As had occurred at lunchtime, it seemed their rare periods of more moderate conversation were fated to be short-lived before they reverted to arguments, and so it was for the remainder of the evening, Marti's feelings becoming even more incensed as she climbed reluctantly into her unrolled swag, and when she found the ground as hard and punishing on her unaccustomed muscles as she had envisaged, sleep was exceptionally difficult to come by.

CHAPTER FOUR

THE following morning Marti was awake early, not merely because she hadn't managed to sleep much at all—even when she had done, it had been fitful due to her tossing and turning in a vain effort to find at least one reasonably comfortable position—but mainly because a pair of blue-winged kookaburras came to alight in one of the trees beside their camp. Their ensuing chorus, more of a screaming parody of their larger, brown-and-white cousins' raucous laughter, made any chance of further sleep extremely remote. The species weren't known as the bushman's clock for nothing.

Still, she made no move to rise. In fact, she began to doubt she could do so even had she wanted to, for with every movement her whole body now seemed to scream in protest due to its cavalier treatment. Not altogether to her surprise, though, she did notice before determinedly re-closing her eyes that Farrell's swag had already been neatly re-rolled and stacked against the Land Cruiser ready for loading, although there was no sign of the man himself, and she presumed him to be down at the river. She should have known he'd have to rise with the damned birds, just like every other farmer, she scowled.

'Come on, Marti, out of there! We haven't got all day!'

All too soon Farrell's peremptory voice was penetrating her drowsy brain, the accompanying slap on her rear bringing forth an involuntary exclamation of pain and furious indignation. 'You ever do that again and it'll be at your own risk, Farrell Stephens!' she blazed, pushing herself up on one elbow and brushing her tumbled hair from her face. 'While as for not having all day, heavens above, it's still the middle of the night!' Her eyes lifted skywards eloquently to where the sun was only just beginning to make an appearance.

'Yeah, well, you may be able to sleep till mid-morning at home, sweetheart, but not here, so on your feet,' he returned insistently. 'The billy will soon be boiling.'

'Oh, beaut!' she quipped facetiously. She had tried another mug of the black tea last night but was still no closer to acquiring a taste for it than she had been previously. 'That's an inducement not to get up, if anything is!'

'Except that if you don't, I may just be tempted to haul you out myself,' he bent to drawl with lazily ominous intent as he passed on his way to get something from the vehicle.

'You may have to anyway,' she dared to retort. 'One night in this,' indicating the bed-roll derisively, 'and I feel as if every part of me has been crippled for life!'

'Apart from your tongue, obviously!' he gibed in mocking accents on his way back to the newly lit fire.

Marti turned her back on him, ostensibly in a huff, but in reality to hide the ungovernable grin that began pulling at her lips as her customary sense of humour—which, under normal circumstances, wasn't usually far from the surface—unexpectedly came to the fore. It also made her many aches and pains seem a little easier to bear somehow.

Once they were back on the road, as Farrell had

predicted, the further north they travelled the worse the road, and the shaking taken by the Land Cruiser, became. Once more there were many rivers to cross, Marti discovered, some by low, adzed bridges—sturdy examples from a bygone age—others by way of the bed of the river itself, the countryside between mainly consisting of thick forests of blood-woods or ti-tree flats dotted with red and grey termite mounds, the edges of the north/south-constructed magnetic variety seeming on occasion to be knife-sharp.

'Back to these properties again,' she began on one occasion as they started to pick up speed after having stopped beside another vehicle pulled up on the side of the road to enquire if any help was required. It was just the legendary courtesy of outback motorists, she had realised on having seen him do the same the day before, a case of everyone being willing to help everyone else in such remote areas, because no one ever knew when they might need assistance in turn. 'Do they have names, by the way?'

Farrell nodded. 'The larger of the two is Leawarra, the other Raeburn.'

'And do you also think they could both be viable propositions?'

He merely gave a shrug of his wide shoulders, his lips taking on an oblique tilt. 'You're asking *my* opinion?' he countered pointedly.

If he did but know she had a great deal more than that to ask of him, but like the day before, she judged it wasn't the appropriate time, especially not when everything just about had to be shouted in order to be heard. 'Why not?' She hunched a shoulder herself now. 'As you've apparently been delegated to show them to me it's you I'll have to ask any questions of then, and doubtlessly you know the area as well as

Uncle Vern does, anyhow.' Pausing, she flashed him an expressive glance. 'Or are you nervous of committing yourself?'

'Not particularly,' he drawled, the look he slanted her in return even more meaningful than her own had been. 'I was merely surprised, that's all. To date, you haven't exactly given any indication that my opinions were ever likely to be welcome.'

'Probably because, to date, all your opinions— judgments, more like—have been of a personal nature, and highly uncomplimentary at that!' she burst out compulsively. Then she went on swiftly in her most business-like manner, 'However, that's neither here nor there at the moment. This is different, and a subject you *are* familiar with.' She still couldn't refrain from the gentle gibe. 'So, do you consider them both viable propositions?'

After another brief but significant look, he nodded. 'With the right men in charge—as I said yesterday.'

'One man couldn't run both?' she enquired, noting his use of the plural.

'He could, although it would involve a lot more work, naturally—particularly as they're in different areas—and he'd definitely need a reliable overseer at the other one. All of which is still quite possible, of course. I was merely meaning if they were run as separate entities.'

'I see,' Marti acknowledged thoughtfully. 'And if you had to choose between the two, which one would you select?'

'On your father's behalf, or my own?' he surprised her by asking.

'Why should there be a difference?' she frowned.

'To accommodate different priorities,' Farrell supplied with a wry twist to his lips. 'Investors like prompt returns, and since Raeburn would produce those more readily at this point of time, all things considered I would probably recommend that as the best prospect for your father. Leawarra, on the other hand, despite being far more run-down at present, I'm inclined to think could have the best long-term potential, and consequently that's the one I'd be more likely to choose for myself.'

'So overall, Leawarra is actually the better property, then?'

'Since I've no proof to back up what, at this stage, are really only instincts on my part regarding Leawarra . . .' he flexed an implicit shoulder, 'in the final analysis there could turn out to be little to choose between them.'

'But your personal preference is still for Leawarra?'

'Uh-huh!' Although lazily voiced the expression carried a wealth of decisive conviction nonetheless.

Sitting silent for the moment, Marti assimilated the information contemplatively. 'Wouldn't size also have some bearing on it, though?' she queried at length. She would have thought it did.

'Not in this instance,' he rejected, shaking his head. 'Once again, with one being just over a thousand square miles and the other slightly under, the difference between them is neglible.'

'Mmm, I guess so,' she acceded slowly. Put like that the difference did seem minimal, whereas the acreages her father had mentioned had made it sound much greater. And with her present stock of questions seemingly exhausted—what other enquiries was someone as ignorant of the land as she was supposed to make?—she sighed and turned her attention elsewhere.

The landscape was now becoming more tropical

with each mile that passed, she noted, and not unappreciatively, she realised, in spite of her inclinations to have it otherwise. Attractive pandanus and grass-trees were beginning to make increasing appearances among the other growth, the ubiquitous termite mounds more prolific and growing taller. The common factor was the dust. It carpeted not only the road but the trees lining it as well. Every vehicle that passed, and there had been an unexpected number of them, bountifully added to it from the choking clouds they trailed behind them.

Eventually, though, late in the morning, and after lurching across a range of granite-ridged hills where the continuous dips and rises had given the sensation of being on a giant, never-ending roller-coaster, they made it into the small township of Coen, and when Farrell brought them to a halt, saying he had something to pick up from the garage, Marti was even more pleased at the opportunity to leave the vehicle for a while than she had been the day before.

She felt as if she had been battered from pillar to post, and she wasn't at all surprised to learn that some passengers had been known to suffer strains and even dislocations during their journeys.

'No wonder Toyota use Australia to road-test their four-wheel drives,' she groaned with feeling on alighting. 'If they can survive that, they can survive anything!'

Farrell didn't reply, his lips merely taking on an oblique curve which promptly had her casting him an initially suspicious, then eye-widening look of disbelief.

'There's worse to come?' she deduced on a rising note of despair.

The slope to his mouth became a little more

pronounced. 'I haven't even used four-wheel-drive yet, sweetheart.' Then, as if unexpectedly taking pity on her, or wearying of her complaints, he said, 'Although from here to the airfield north of town the road's pretty good, and since we turn off shortly thereafter on to Tullagindi's own roads, I think you can rest assured that the worst is over for today at least.'

'Certainly not before time,' she still grumbled as they turned for the café in the town's wide and sparsely occupied main street. 'And if there's an airfield here, why couldn't I have been collected there instead of being subjected to that tortuous drive?'

'Mainly because *I* happened to be in Cairns at that particular time, but also because it was doubtful whether anyone could be spared for that purpose due to the preparations for the rodeo. The immediate days beforehand, especially, are rather busy ones for everyone on the station,' he clipped out in satirical tones. 'Besides, you're forgetting your father's wish that you see something of the area, aren't you?'

'I would have enjoyed it more from the air!' she had no hesitation in retorting as they entered the building.

From the expression on Farrell's face it was evident he would have found it more enjoyable too, but deeming it judicious not to comment on the fact, nor, inexplicably, even inclined to take the matter further herself, she sought a less contentious subject once their order had been given and they had returned to the table outside to await its delivery.

'Whereabouts did my father live? Do you know?' she asked quietly as she scanned the few houses that seemed to dot the area haphazardly. She found it hard to imagine that she too might have grown up in this isolated outpost if her parent's highly successful propensity for wheeling and dealing hadn't had him gravitating to the city.

'Not exactly, because it was the house burning down and,' he paused slightly, 'his mother's resultant death, that apparently precipitated his departure. I understand it used to be somewhere up on that hill, though.' He indicated one of the lower ridges that surrounded the town.

'I see,' she acknowledged quietly. 'I suppose the town must have held just too many sad memories for him at the time, after having lost his father in an accident too only a few years earlier.'

'More than likely,' Farrell conceded, nodding his thanks and passing a few words with the young girl, whom he obviously knew, who brought out a tray with their tea and some biscuits on it. 'Although he evidently still kept in touch with people here, even so. In person too, in later years, of course.'

'Something I've never really been able to understand, I must admit,' Marti suddenly found herself confessing. She made herself go on, nevertheless. 'And even sitting here now, seeing the place for the first time, I still can't understand why it should apparently have such a hold on him, or have made such an impression on him. God knows, there's little enough here.'

'Then maybe it was simply a case of quality rather than quantity,' he put forward with heavy irony. 'Did you ever think of that?'

'Yes, much as it may surprise you, I did!' she retorted, wishing she had kept her thoughts to herself. 'Only . . .'

'Only living the superficial existence you do, you couldn't understand how that could possibly be, either, I suppose!' he inserted.

'No, now that you come to mention it, I couldn't!' she fired back, defending herself with sarcasm.

'Well, perhaps if you'd made the effort to accompany Harry on a couple of his trips up here, you might have found out! But then, I guess that really was expecting too much from someone who only has a nodding relationship with reality!'

'Only according to you!'

'*And* your father, presumably!'—succinctly.

Marti caught at her lip with even white teeth, abruptly aware of just how disappointed in her her father evidently must have been for him to have insisted that she make this visit, together with all it entailed, and yet all the time she had believed neither of her parents would have found fault with her in any regard. The fact that her father had—and maybe even her mother too, for she had been quite adamant as well that she comply with her father's wishes, Marti now recalled—left her feeling as if she had been suddenly cut adrift, and not quite certain of anything any more.

'Yes, and my father, apparently,' she conceded finally, throatily, the sun making her eyes sting as her averted gaze took in the town basking in the shimmering heat. When she turned back again, there was a protective defiance in the set of her finely formed features. 'But now, having successfully managed not only to ruin my day completely but also ensure I derive no enjoyment whatsoever from the remainder of my visit, I hope you're satisfied at last, and the subject can be dropped once and for all!'

Farrell's jaw tightened. 'Don't go venting your annoyance on me just because I made you see the truth for once, Marti, or you could really find all hell starting to break loose!' he warned grimly. 'In any event, I wasn't under the impression you anticipated

finding *anything* pleasurable in this visit of yours!' A
dark brow quirked goadingly.

Nor had she originally, but didn't allow that to stop
her from snapping, 'Which simply proves you don't
know as much about me as you obviously, mistakenly,
think!' She began rising to her feet, experiencing an
imperative need for time alone in order to collect her
fragmented thoughts and feelings. 'And now I'm sure
you'll have no objections if I wait for you in the
Cruiser.'

'Oh, don't be so immature!' he immediately rasped,
a snaking hand capturing her arm and forcing her
inexorably back to the seat again. 'You've had a loss
for once in your life, so now you're going to take your
marbles and go home, are you?' His eyes locked
derisively with hers. 'Just drink your tea, for God's
sake!'

'No!' she refused fiercely, struggling to escape the
grip that still kept her restrained. 'And let go of me!'
Her voice rose slightly as a kind of panic began to set
in. She just couldn't think straight while he continued
to condemn and mock her at will. 'I want to return to
the car, and I—I'm going to return t-to . . . oh, damn
you, Farrell! Damn you for an arrogant, interfering
creep!' she choked bitterly as she felt humiliating
tears start to spill on to her lashes, and her head bowed
defeatedly. No man had ever succeeded in actually
making her cry before, and that it should be this one
who had, made it just that much more difficult to
accept.

'Oh, hell!' Farrell released a heavy breath and,
dragging off his hat, scrubbed a hand through his hair
savagely. Then, leaning forward, he caught her chin
and dragged it upwards. 'And don't you know better
than to cry when your face is covered in dust,' he

stated rather than asked in a partly wry, partly rueful voice as he began repairing the damage with a handkerchief he took from his pocket, and with a surprisingly gentle touch.

After one futile attempt to pull away, Marti submitted to his ministrations with a dejected acquiescence. But when he had finished he remained close, his gaze watchful.

'I'm sorry,' he sighed. 'I guess it really wasn't my right to involve myself as I did.'

Surprised at the apology—she hadn't thought him the type—Marti merely hunched a slender shoulder as she half turned to stare across the road at the masses of large, rich yellow, trumpet-shaped flowers on the allamanda vine that climbed over the old wooden store opposite. 'It doesn't matter,' she claimed tonelessly. 'I suppose the truth has to be faced some time, even by spoilt, rich kids like me.'

'Marti!' he half frowned, half remonstrated.

'Well, that is how you think of me, isn't it?' she queried in the same dull manner as she swung back to face him.

'Yeah, although I certainly never expected to have to add self-pitying to the list as well!' Farrell bit out.

As it happened, self-pity was the furthest thing from her mind, but in the distracted mood she was in, Marti wasn't averse to fostering that belief if that was how he chose to view it. 'Just another instance of your not knowing me as well as you thought, perhaps?' she suggested impassively, picking up her cup.

'So it would appear!' He broke a biscuit in half with a force she suspected he would have preferred to use on her neck.

A couple of hours later, and with very few further

words exchanged between them, Marti realised their
journey would soon be completed as definite signs of
habitation began to make an appearance in the form of
tracts of cleared land surrounded by wire-strung
fences. For the most part it was still quite thickly
timbered country they passed through, although the
eucalypts were now interspersed with red and peach-
coloured flowering kurrajongs as well as golden
grevillaeas.

Then all at once she could see the homestead before
them. Set in a huge clearing, it dominated the
customary conglomeration of outbuildings, holding-
yards, and loading-ramp situated a few hundred yards
away to one side, a red earth airstrip stretching into
the distance on the other.

The house itself was long and set high for coolness,
the upper encircling balcony balustraded and totally
enclosed with insect screening. A lawn at the front of
the building—edged by a variety of hibiscus, Bangkok
roses, and bougainvillaeas—plus a couple of tall,
heavily laden mango-trees to provide shade, completed
the picture.

The sound of the Cruiser's approach must have
carried clearly in the hot, still atmosphere, Marti
deduced, because even before they had come to a halt
at the gate that gave entrance to the homestead
complex—Marti willingly doing the honours of
opening and then closing it again behind the vehicle
now that she could look forward to a respite from the
dust and constant shaking—figures had appeared from
within the house and a couple of barking, blue and
black-coated cattle dogs had bounded up from the
direction of the yards.

'Marti! It's lovely to see you again,' Farrell's mother
greeted her warmly immediately she alighted; her

husband reserving his until he had quietened the noisy welcome, or warning, Marti wasn't sure which, being given by the dogs and then summarily despatched them back to where they had come from with a few commanding words.

'Aunt Roma—Uncle Vern,' she acknowledged in turn with a half-smile. 'It's nice to see you both again too.'

'She means, especially as it relieves her of my constant company for a while,' put in Farrell drily, who was himself being eagerly greeted by a pretty young girl of some seventeen years with dark curly hair and sparkling brown eyes.

Marti didn't comment, in spite of agreeing wholeheartedly with the sentiment expressed, and it was left to Roma Stephens to eye her son dubiously. 'I hope that doesn't mean you didn't make exceptions for poor Marti, Farrell. After all, you know she's not used to making such journeys, and *I* know only too well your reluctance to stop once you get going.' She turned to the girl beside her. 'I can understand how you must feel. It is a long, hot uncomfortable drive, and I bet he didn't even stop in Laura or Coen so you could have a drink and something of a rest.' She flashed her son a look of fond exasperation this time.

'Actually, we did stop in Coen,' said Marti. She just wished they hadn't.

'Mmm, I had something to pick up there.' Farrell had no compunction in explaining the real reason.

'Oh, they'd got those parts in, then? That's good,' his father applauded, his concern obviously for the more important aspects of the matter.

'While I'm forgetting my manners,' interposed Roma Stephens with an apologetic smile for her guest. 'You haven't met Elizabeth yet, have you?' She called

the younger girl over. 'Elizabeth, I'd like you to meet
Marti—Martine—Grayson. Elizabeth Woodfield,' she
concluded for Marti's benefit.

'Hello,' acknowledged the dark-haired girl with a
noticeable lack of enthusiasm, the full-lipped, wide
smile that had been turned on Farrell totally absent now.

'I'm pleased to meet you too,' returned Marti a
touch sardonically. Good heavens, the girl was glaring
at her as if she were a rival, she suddenly realised. But
for whom, Farrell? If she only knew, she was welcome
to him as far as Marti was concerned, but simultaneously, did *his* tastes run to adolescents?
Involuntarily, she cast a covert glance in his direction,
but finding him, along with his father, starting to
unload the vehicle, shrugged indifferently. So what if
they did, it was nothing to her.

'Yes, well, shall we adjourn inside now?' Roma
Stephens smiled encouragingly, evidently not
altogether unaware of the by-play that had taken
place. 'I'm sure you could still do with a nice cool
drink and something to eat even if you did stop in
town. And as a matter of fact, there's someone upstairs
waiting to see you who's an old friend of yours,
apparently. We only found out about it today while we
were talking over lunch.'

'An old friend of mine?' Marti frowned in surprise
as the two of them made their way up the steps to the
verandah, Elizabeth having elected to remain down-
stairs—with Farrell, of course, Marti noted with a
grimace.

'Mmm, isn't that nice?' Roma chattered on in her
usual kindly fashion. 'Now you won't feel quite so
among strangers, will you?'

Marti merely half smiled politely, wondering who
on earth it could be, although it didn't take long to

find out for, on reaching the upstairs verandah, she was soon being introduced to the three women seated there around a glass-topped table. The first was Lucy Woodfield, Elizabeth's stepmother; the second, Alison, the flame-haired young wife of Braden, Farrell's brother; while the third, an attractive-looking girl of much Marti's own age, indeed required no introduction.

'Hi! Long time no see,' she greeted Marti with a wide smile.

'Jess? Jessica Dunbar!' Marti stared at her in amazement on recognising an old classmate from her boarding-school days who, although not having been one of her closest companions—their backgrounds, and therefore their interests had really been too dissimilar for that—had still been a welcomed friend all the same. She took the chair proffered beside the tawny-haired girl. 'What are you doing here! I thought your family's property was way out west.' Her eyes began to widen expressively. 'Or don't tell me you came all this distance just for the rodeo!'

'Oh, no!' the other girl disclaimed with a laugh. 'That place was sold when Mum married Roy, Elizabeth's father, shortly after I finished school.' This explained why Lucy Woodfield had somehow seemed familiar, Marti supposed. She had probably seen her before at some end-of-the-year school prize-giving function or other. It also reminded her that Jessica's own father had been killed in a tractor accident early in their school days. 'We live on the Peninsula now. Not all that far from here, as a matter of fact.'

'I see,' nodded Marti. 'And do you prefer it here to out west?' a sudden impulsive and unexplained curiosity had her enquiring.

'Oh, you know me,' Jessica half laughed wryly. 'Anywhere suits me, as long as it's not the city.'

'We might also add, the more so now that the property next door to Fernlea has a new and very personable young manager in charge,' inserted Alison with a bantering grin.

'Oh!' smiled Marti understandingly, assuming Fernlea to be the property where Jessica now lived, and cast that girl a sideways glance. 'So that's how things are, is it?'

'Sort of,' Jessica allowed with a somewhat self-conscious lift of her shoulder, sending a mock-threatening glance in Alison's direction. 'Not that there's anything definite in it as yet, of course.' She steered the conversation away from herself quickly. 'So how about you? There's no particular man in your life at the moment?'

Marti shook her head. 'No, no one special. I'm still playing the field, so to speak.'

'But I thought I read in the social columns of one of the papers we get that you were on the point of becoming engaged,' put in Roma Stephens on a surprised note.

'Just being seen with the same man on more than two occasions is usually sufficient to have that kind of rumour circulating,' Marti advised, her lips twisting ruefully. 'To date, I think the columnists have had me on the verge of getting married something like four times, and yet not once have I even been considering it.'

'That could be embarrassing,' frowned Lucy.

'It was the first time.' The agreement was expressed with whimsical feeling. 'Particularly since the fellow in question seemed to think it signified my approval for the arrangement. After a while, you learn to ignore any such reports, though.'

Roma clucked sympathetically and started to rise. 'However, you must still be famished, and since you've met everyone now, perhaps you'd like to come with me and I'll get you some lunch and something to drink,' she smiled.

'I'd prefer a wash first, if I may,' put forward Marti with an explicit grimace for her covering of dust as she too rose upright.

'Oh, yes, of course,' her request was granted immediately. 'Although you needn't feel at all uncomfortable about it, you know. We all realise just how unavoidable it is, believe me.'

This statement was soundly endorsed by all others present prior to Jessica offering, 'If you like, I'll show Marti where the bathroom is, Roma. And her bedroom.'

'Thank you, Jess, that's very thoughtful of you,' the older woman accepted. 'I'll just get along to the kitchen, then, and leave you to show Marti where the dining-room is too afterwards, all right?'

Both girls nodded their compliance, and a few minutes later Jessica was opening the door to a comfortably furnished and attractively decorated room that led from a wide hall that appeared to run the length of the house. 'Bedroom,' she advised laconically. 'And that's our bathroom across there,' indicating another doorway on the opposite side of the hall. 'At the moment it's only Mum, Elizabeth, you and I who'll be using it, but come Friday and the house starts to fill, it will be a different matter, naturally. In fact, by then we'll have to be sharing bedrooms as well in order to fit as many in as possible. That is, the women, at least. The men either sleep on the verandah or outside.' She paused. 'Roma was saying at lunch that she thought she might put you in

with Elizabeth and me since you and I know each
other. I hope that's okay with you.'

'Of course,' Marti felt obliged to grant, despite not
being used to it, nor having expected to share her
bedroom with anyone; not that she really objected to
sharing with the other girl. It was more her young
stepsister she had reservations about. 'It will be just
like being back at school.'

'Only without a dragon of a Matron ready and
willing to haul you over the coals at every opportunity,'
Jessica laughed.

Instead she had Farrell Stephens taking on the part,
said Marti to herself, even as she joined in with the
other girl's amusement.

Presently, feeling considerably fresher after having
removed the day's accumulation of dust from her skin,
if not her hair and clothes, Marti rejoined her friend
and together they made their way along the passage to
the dining-room with Jessica pointing out salient
aspects as they went.

'I gather you've been here a number of times,'
Marti commented humorously.

Jessica nodded. 'Every year for the rodeo since we
moved to Fernlea.' She hesitated. 'And in that regard
I must admit I was, to put it mildly, somewhat
astounded when I discovered you would also be
attending this year. Don't tell me that after all this
time you've suddenly had a change of heart
concerning the country?' Her dark-blue eyes twinkled
teasingly.

'No, not really,' Marti disclosed on a dry note,
dismissing those momentary lapses during the journey
when she had found the scenery quite to her liking. 'It
was my father's idea that I come in his stead this year,
because he was unable to make the journey himself.'

'That sounds more like it,' chuckled Jessica. 'I was sorry to hear about his operation, though, and that he wouldn't be coming this year. I like your father, he's a good sport, and he really joins in everything while he's here.'

Suddenly realising her friend obviously knew her father quite well from his regular trips to the rodeo, Marti gazed at her curiously. 'Although it's funny that he never mentioned having met you here. Didn't you tell him that we went to school together?'

'There didn't seem any point,' Jessica shrugged casually. 'Knowing your feelings regarding the bush, I doubted whether there was any likelihood of your changing your mind and coming one time, simply because I happened to be here.'

And neither probably would she have done, conceded Marti honestly, that thought, plus the other girl's so very philosophical attitude, abruptly making her feel slightly discomfited. Had she truly become so self-absorbed, as Farrell had alleged, that she wouldn't willingly inconvenience herself for anyone, parent or friend, any more?

'Well, I'm here now,' she responded at last with deliberate lightness. 'And we've probably both got a lot of gossip to catch up on. Did you know that Roxanne Kingston-Clarke is getting divorced, again?'

'Again?' Jessica repeated in surprise as they turned into the dining-room. 'I didn't even know she'd been married.'

'Oh, yes, three times, in fact. Not that any of her marriages last long, but I think she set a record with this one. It survived for a whole six days.'

Due mainly to Jessica's pleasant company, Marti was able to relax and enjoy the remainder of the afternoon, but dinner soon proved to be another matter. Farrell's presence merely served to remind her of their last confrontation in Coen, and thus its dismaying cause, with the result that she immediately became withdrawn as she struggled for some perspective on the matter. Then too, there was Elizabeth, obviously infatuated with Farrell, whose side she continued to cling to like fly-paper, Marti noticed, and was just as evidently not prepared to show the newcomer in their midst the least civility, let alone amiability.

'I'm so glad you were *finally* able to make it back in time for the muster tomorrow,' Elizabeth began with pointed emphasis almost as soon as they were all seated at the table for the meal, her sparkling eyes concentrated in Farrell's direction. 'I really pestered Mum and Dad into arriving a day earlier than usual just so we could take part as well, and it would have been the absolute pits if you'd then missed it because of being delayed for so long.'

'There wasn't much chance of that happening,' Farrell shrugged lightly. 'If there had been, I would simply have driven straight through without stopping.'

This disclosure had Elizabeth promptly beaming, and apparently assuming he had meant he hadn't wanted to miss her company on the muster either. Marti wasn't so sure, particularly since she doubted that, as the other girl had evidently arrived earlier than usual, he would even have been aware of her likely participation.

'Talking about the muster, though,' joined in Trent, Jessica's tall, pleasant-faced older brother, 'perhaps Marti would like to come out with us tomorrow too.' He sent an enquiring smile across the table.

About to decline, hastily—plodding through the bush all day after lumbering cattle was definitely not her idea of pleasure—Marti nonetheless wasn't afforded the opportunity to do so due to Elizabeth's forestalling her.

'Oh, don't be a moron, Trent! She probably can't even ride!' that girl scoffed. 'Martine lives in Brisbane, remember?'

'So?' he shrugged imperturbably. 'Even people who live in cities can still go riding, you know.'

'And of course Marti can ride!' added Jessica in squashing tones, much to her friend's regret. 'We used to go riding sometimes at the weekends when we were at school. Didn't we?' She sought confirmation from Marti.

'Well, yes,' the corroboration was reluctantly given. 'Although . . .'

'There, you see!' Jessica interrupted with a wry look at her stepsister. She turned back to the girl beside her almost immediately. 'So you'll come with us, won't you? It should be quite an exciting day, and I'll even pick your mount out for you myself, if you like.' An engaging grin caught at her lips.

Marti half smiled wanly in return. It was true she could ride, and even enjoyed it, but at the same time a couple of turns around the park wasn't exactly on a par with a whole day's mustering.

'Yes, you'd better make sure it's one she doesn't have *too* much trouble handling, if she is going to come,' sniped Elizabeth, her dissatisfaction at the prospect quite plain. 'There won't be time for anyone to be fussing around her all day, ensuring she doesn't fall off, or something.'

And certainly least of all by you, thought Marti, becoming a trifle nettled by the continual disparagement.

Roy Woodfield, the dark-haired girl's normally

jovial father, must have noticed this, because he promptly fixed his daughter with a reproving frown and censured, 'Elizabeth! That's quite enough!'

Far from appearing chastised, though, she merely gave her dark curls a defiant toss. 'Well, since she's obviously never been on a muster before,' with a scornful twist to her mouth, 'she probably *won't* be able to keep up, and she's just hoping that by appearing reluctant everyone will make allowances for her!'

'Mmm, we can all see how successful she's been where you're concerned,' put in Jessica, drily explicit. She gave a deprecating shake of her head. 'God, you can be a poisonous, spoilt brat at times, Elizabeth!'

'Oh, yes, I might have known you'd feel obliged to come to her defence, Jessica! After all, she's your friend!' came the hot retort. 'But someone had to tell her the facts, and *I* wasn't afraid of being that person!'

'As you've made abundantly clear, unfortunately, and once too often!' Her father's voice sounded in an ominous bark. 'I said that was enough, and I meant it! Even if you do fail to realise it, you're causing embarrassment to everyone else at the table.'

With her lips still pressing into a mutinous line, Elizabeth did at least condescend to glance towards Roma and Vern Stephens. I'm sorry,' she apologised, but in a manner that still managed to convey more resentment than remorse as she at last fell silent and returned her attention to her meal

They all did for a time, until Farrell chose to re-open the subject by enquiring sardonically of Marti, 'So do you intend to take part or not?'

This question earned him a fulminating glare—he knew damned well it held no attraction for her whatsoever!—but while Elizabeth's remarks continued to rankle, the lazily mocking look in his thickly framed, hazel eyes was sufficient to have her conversely, impetuously, reversing her decision.

'Of course,' she replied in lightly amused tones as if the issue had never been in doubt. 'It sounds as though it could be a most—umm—enlightening experience.'

'Oh, that's good!' Jessica approved immediately. 'I thought for a while there that you meant to give the idea the thumbs down.'

From the expression on Elizabeth's face, it was clear she wished she had.

'And don't you worry, we'll see that no cantankerous old scrubbers get anywhere near you, no matter what Elizabeth says,' joked Trent.

Marti's eyes widened. 'Cantankerous old scrubbers?' she hazarded somewhat perplexedly.

'Mmm, with some parts of just about all properties on the Peninsula, Tullagindi included, being all but inaccessible to both men on horseback and helicopters, there's always a few cattle that manage to evade our annual musters, and they simply revert to the wild,' Braden now entered the conversation to inform her. 'Consequently, when their run of luck does eventually come to an end, they're mean and cranky and don't hesitate to show it, especially to those who curtail that freedom.'

'Oh!' she nodded faintly. 'Although those aren't the animals you're hoping to muster tomorrow, I presume?' She sincerely hoped not!

'Why, thinking of changing your mind if they are?'

The lazily drawled provocation could only have come from one person, and she faced him with a resolutely elevated chin. 'Not at all,' she denied valiantly. Since she was already beginning to rue her impulsive agreement, she only wished she could! 'I was merely enquiring.'

'Then the answer is, no, we will not be bull-running, expressly, tomorrow. We normally use vehicles fitted with special equipment for that, in any case,' he divulged wryly. 'However, should we happen to come across one, anyway . . .' He shrugged and left the sentence meaningfully unfinished.

Nodding once more, Marti deliberately dropped her gaze and continued with her meal, wondering why in heaven's name she had stupidly allowed herself to be goaded into joining the muster in the first place. It wasn't as if it interested her at all, nor had she experienced any sudden, overwhelming desire to go riding, but surely it should have required more than one malicious seventeen-year-old, and a purposely satirical remark, to have provoked her into doing so!

It was a complete about-face from her usual cool-headed decisions, and she was no more reconciled to either that knowledge, or the thought of taking part in the morrow's activities, by the time she went to bed that evening.

CHAPTER FIVE

THE following morning Marti wasn't any more enthusiastic about the muster than she had been the night before, and especially not after having been roused from her bed by Jessica before it was even light.

Outfitted in jeans, boots, and a hat provided by her friend and Alison Stephens jointly—she hadn't brought any riding-gear with her—she had then partaken of breakfast with the others in a kind of benumbed silence, her whole system seemingly in a state of shocked rebellion at being forced into action at such an ungodly hour. She hadn't even had to rise this early when she had camped with Farrell, she groaned.

Notwithstanding her body's feeling of outrage, however, from the talk going on around her she did find herself making some unintentional and un-expected discoveries concerning the people at the table with her, and life on the Peninsula too.

For a start, it had very readily become apparent that Tullagindi was truly a working cattle-station, with the emphasis on 'working', and where every member of the family was expected to, and did, make a distinct contribution—much as Farrell had once intimated. A private, thousand-square-mile empire it might have been, but there were no airs of the wealthy elite practised here. They were simply the down-to-earth people of the bush her father had so often told, or attempted to tell, her about.

They were independent, self-sufficinet, and pos-

sessed of an amazing initiative brought about by the
necessity of living an often hard, always isolated life in
a still virtually unexplored region, who seemed to
thrive on challenges, but clearly wouldn't have
exchanged their individualistic lifestyle no matter
what; a lifestyle that was also more than likely
responsible for all the men seeming to be made from
the same mould, Marti had already decided wryly the
previous evening on first meeting Roy Woodfield and
Trent Dunbar. For like Farrell, Braden, and their
father, they too were tall, large-framed men, their
bodies made hard with muscle through physical
labour, their strong masculine features tanned uni-
formly to the same dark hue, and once again like
Farrell, they all exuded an aura of capability, of
security, and of calm but indisputable self-assurance
and authority.

Put them all together and you'd need a map and a
water bottle to get around them, she assessed drily on
feeling herself positively dwarfed by them as they all
saddled up after breakfast. Her only consolation was
that neither Jessica, an inch or so taller than herself,
nor Elizabeth, about an inch shorter, looked any more
significant beside them than she did.

The sun was only just starting to appear above the
horizon when they began heading away from the
yards, along with half a dozen or so ringers—as
stockmen were called in Queensland, due to their
practice in the days of droving of 'ringing' the cattle
when camped at night to ensure they remained calm—
and a similar number of eager cattle dogs.

The horses, fresh and frisky at that hour of the day,
snorted and curvetted in the cool morning air,
although Marti was rather relieved to note that the
mount that, in the end, Farrell had selected for her

Say **YES** to Romance

AND YOU'LL GET:

4 FREE BOOKS
A LIGHTED MAKEUP MIRROR AND BRUSH KIT
A FREE SURPRISE GIFT

**NO RISK
NO OBLIGATION
NO STRINGS
NO KIDDING**

EXCITING DETAILS INSIDE

Say **YES** to free gifts worth over $20.00

Say YES to a rendezvous with romance, and you'll get 4 classic love stories—FREE! You'll get a lighted makeup mirror and brush kit—FREE! And you'll get a delightful surprise—FREE! These gifts carry a total value of over $20.00—but you can have them without spending even a penny!

MONEY-SAVING HOME DELIVERY!

Say YES to Harlequin's Reader Service, and you'll enjoy the convenience of previewing six brand-new books delivered right to your home months before they appear in stores. Each book is yours for only $1.66—29¢ less than the retail price.

SPECIAL EXTRAS—FREE!

You'll get our monthly newsletter, *Heart to Heart*—the indispensable insider's look at our most popular writers and their upcoming novels. Now you can have a behind-the-scenes look at the fascinating world of Harlequin! You'll also get additional free gifts from time to time as a token of our appreciation for being a home subscriber.

Say YES to a Harlequin love affair. Complete, detach and mail your Free Offer Card today!

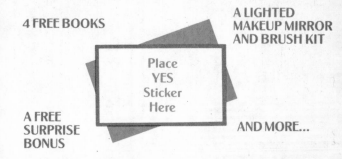

BUSINESS REPLY CARD

First Class   Permit No. 717   Buffalo, NY

Postage will be paid by addressee

Harlequin Reader Service

901 Fuhrmann Blvd.,
P.O. Box 1394
Buffalo, NY 14240-9963

NO POSTAGE
NECESSARY
IF MAILED
IN THE
UNITED STATES

wasn't quite as keen to display his high spirits as some of the others were. It allowed her more of an opportunity to look about her, and after one such scanning glance over the party she turned to Jessica, who was alongside her, with a frown.

'Where's Alison? I can't see her anywhere. In fact, I can't remember seeing her since breakfast.'

'No, you wouldn't. Alison never comes mustering, or even does much riding at all, for that matter,' Jessica relayed casually. 'With her very fair skin she just ends up looking like a lobster unless she covers herself up to such an extent that it takes all the enjoyment out of it, anyway.'

'I see,' nodded Marti, thinking the absent girl lucky to have such an excuse. She only wished she had thought to use it herself, although in view of the way in which her own skin was already taking on a warmly golden colour as a result of their stops during the drive from Cairns—at such latitudes very little exposure was necessary to have a noticeable effect—she doubted such a ploy would have succeeded.

With the yards well behind them, the horses were urged into a steady, ground-covering canter past stately gums and thick melaleucas, around termite mounds that towered above man and horse, and through drying undergrowth and tall grass.

'Where are we going? Do you know?' Marti called across to Jessica after a time.

'Somewhere around the Five Mile Yards, I think. I gather there's been no mustering done in that area at all yet this year.'

Marti gave a sickly smile in acknowledgment. Well, that should ensure it was an extra long day, she despaired, and she suspected her muscles were already preparing to protest. After all, it was at least six months since she had done any riding. With a sigh, she tried pretending she was somewhere else.

By mid-morning the muster was well under way, the riders spread far apart now, stockwhips cracking in the increasingly hot, still air to spur into joining the multiplying herd those groups of cattle that showed inclinations to remain where they were, the dogs eagerly lending their assistance wherever it was required, and even where it wasn't.

Marti and Jessica had been given the task of tailing the slow but steadily moving herd at a walk, much to Marti's relief, for she was now wishing she hadn't been quite so insistent on retaining the shorter stirrup she had been taught to use instead of having it longer like everyone else had. As she could vouch, it didn't make for comfort when long hours were to be spent in the saddle, whereas the others looked far more at ease and relaxed. If they ever did get to stop, she would see about lengthening her own, she decided.

'By the way, I'm sorry for how Elizabeth's behaving towards you, but I shouldn't pay much attention to it all the same, if I were you,' Jessica advised. She gave a wry grin. 'In case you hadn't realised, she's been infatuated with Farrell ever since she was a precocious fourteen-year-old. Now she's an even more precocious seventeen-year-old, she becomes as jealous as a dog with a bone every time an even passably good-looking female comes within coo-ee of him, unfortunately. And you, of course,' with another smile, 'have always been decidedly more than merely passable. Moreover, you also have an extra black mark against you due to him apparently taking you to inspect some properties or the other, because that means you'll be spending more time alone with him.'

'I see,' answered Marti ironically, easing forward in

her saddle in the hope of finding a more comfortable position. If she had followed her companion's advice, she wouldn't now be suffering as she was. 'I deduced she saw me as some kind of rival when we first met, although goodness knows why she would continue to think so. I've hardly spoken to him since we arrived.'

'Mmm, I had noticed that myself,' Jessica averred humorously, sending her an interested glance. 'For any particular reason?'

Involuntarily, Marti's eyes strayed to the subject of their discussion, watching in grudging admiration as he wheeled his mount first one way and then the other to circumvent one particularly recalcitrant steer breaking away from the mob he was bringing in. His movements were spontaneous and so effortless that he simply appeared to be an extension of the horse he rode. Then, determinedly returning her gaze to the girl beside her, she shrugged.

'We just don't see eye to eye, on anything.' And with a little more feeling, 'Your step-sister's welcome to him, as far as I'm concerned!'

'Something I'm sure Elizabeth would be most gratified to hear,' declared Jessica on a dry note. 'However, I somehow doubt whether Farrell would be inclined to endorse the idea.'

To her annoyance, Marti's unaccountable curiosity got the better of her. 'Meaning, he doesn't return her interest?'

A light negative shake of the head. 'I shouldn't think so. Oh, he treats her indulgently enough, which of course Elizabeth contends is proof that he's only waiting for her to gain a little more age before declaring himself, so to speak. But to be honest, I can't really see that being the case. Judging by past experience, I wouldn't say she's his type.'

'Except that she does appear to have the required qualities of being flattering to his ego, submissive to his every whim, and grateful for his slightest attention, of course!' Marti gibed compulsively.

'*If* that was what appealed to him,' came the amused contradiction, followed by an extremely graphic sideways look. 'And don't sound quite so—er—piqued, or I might start getting the wrong idea.'

'*Piqued!*' Marti expostulated scornfully. 'That's utterly ridiculous! Why on earth would I be piqued? I don't even like the man!'

'Because he speaks his mind, whether you like it, or not?'

'Oh, he certainly does that all right!'

'Poor Marti!' Jessica half laughed, half commiserated. 'What a terrible shock it must have been to find someone who wasn't all deference and indulgence where you were concerned.'

'Jess!' Marti stared at her in a mixutre of surprise and dismay. If anyone else had made such a comment she would have considered it malicious, but she knew Jessica had never been like that. She had always dealt with her honestly—one of the reasons she had valued her friendship so highly—and besides, she thought she had detected a degree of pity rather than spite in the other girl's voice, which only added to her disquiet. That anyone might possibly ever feel sorry for her in such a fashion had never entered her mind. 'You surely can't be agreeing with his judgment that—that I've been pampered, and I'm selfish, and—and self-absorbed, and all the rest!' She hesitated, chewing at her lip. 'Can you?'

'So that's what stirred up the hornet's nest, is it? He really let you have it with both barrels, didn't he?' mused Jessica ruefully before replying. 'As for his estimation, well, I don't know that you've ever shown me any signs of the latter two—at least, not intentionally, anyway—but . . .' She began to smile broadly. 'Oh, Marti, of course you've been spoilt. Spoilt rotten, to put it quite bluntly. You always were!'

'Oh!' Marti's expression became even more disconsolate, her friend's 'not intentionally, anyway', doing nothing to alleviate her suddenly stricken conscience. 'I'm sorry,' she sighed. 'I guess I can't have been very nice to know.'

'Oh, of course you were! Otherwise I wouldn't have remained friends with you, would I? Okay, you may have been, well, thoughtless in some ways, but I always considered your good points far outweighed the not-so-good. Much the same as Elizabeth's do. In fact, she reminds me of you quite a lot at times. You've little reason to think so at the moment, I know, but she even has that same ability to take a joke against herself that you used to have, and which I always thought your main saving grace.'

It was a sense of humour that was nowhere in sight, however, as Marti immediately wailed, 'Oh, Jess! Not Elizabeth! She—she's a brat! You said so yourself only last night.'

'Mmm,' was Jessica's only comment, an expressively laconic comment.

A crooked tilt caught at Marti's lips. 'And so am I, is that what you're trying to say?'

There was a slight pause. 'Well, I don't know about nowadays.'

'According to Farrell, I am!' she said acidly.

Jessica eyed her consideringly. 'And were you?'

'Did you really have to ask that?' Pearly white teeth abruptly showed in a wry half-smile. Then pausing,

she released a slow breath, her smile fading. 'Perhaps
. . . probably . . . oh, I don't know! He wasn't precisely
the epitome of gallantry himself?'

'And was that . . .?'

'For God's sake, you two, pay some attention to
what you're doing, will you!' The irate order from
Farrell abruptly slashed through their conversation as
he passed them on his way to the front of the
noticeably spreading mob. 'You're supposed to be
ensuring they stay together, and driving them towards
the yards over there, not allowing them to wander all
over the bloody paddock at will!'

'Oh, dear!' Jessica gulped guiltily and, setting her
heels to her mount's sides, immediately made off at a
gallop in order to wheel one particular group of beasts
back towards the right flank of the main herd.

Marti, meanwhile, supposing it was expect of her to
do the same with the stragglers on the left, set off in
that direction, but without any experience at such
work her efforts proved to be far less successful than
Jessica's. Instead, she somehow managed to have the
cattle scattering further and further afield. The final
straw was when her mount, showing more mastery of
the situation than she did, abruptly reversed direction
in order to block one particular steer's escape, and had
her flying out of the saddle and tumbling to the
ground as a result.

Jessica was the first to reach her as she dragged
herself into a sitting position—her already aching
limbs allowing no fast movement, in any case
—swiftly followed by Farrell and who else but
Elizabeth.

'Are you okay?' quizzed her friend urgently on
hurriedly dismounting.

Marti nodded, her mouth shaping ruefully. 'I think

so. At least everything still seems to move.' Albeit reluctantly! she had to admit.

'That's a relief!' Jessica exhaled thankfully.

'You're all right?' Farrell now asked brusquely in turn as he too reined to a halt and dismounted. Elizabeth remained in the saddle.

'Mmm, she's just a bit shaken, I think, that's all,' Jessica answered on Marti's behalf.

'You're sure?' he still sought verification from Marti directly, his lips taking on an oblique tilt when she nodded. 'Well, don't look so mortified about it, sweetheart.' Bending, he retrieved her hat which had been dislodged during the fall and clamped it back on her head before catching her under the arms and hauling her unceremoniously to her feet. 'It happens to all of us some time or another.' But on noticing her uncontrollable wince as her legs, especially, complained at the abrupt action, he continued on a sharpening note, 'And I thought you said you weren't hurt!'

'I'm not,' she reiterated, if somewhat restively, nor did she intend to give him another opportunity to criticise her by divulging the real reason for her compulsive grimace either. 'I—I just wasn't expecting to be lifted, that's all.'

Momentarily, his measuring gaze remained locked with hers, and then he hunched a dismissive shoulder, beginning to gather his mount's reins into his hand. 'Sorry,' he grunted in a voice totally lacking regret as he swung lithely into the saddle once more. 'So how did it happen, anyway?'

'Oh, it's obvious, isn't it?' interposed Elizabeth who had been surveying the scene scornfully. 'She's just a hopeless rider—as I anticipated last night—and predictably lost all control of her horse! And I might add, that's not all she lost either! Just look at all those cattle *we* now have to muster again!' She flung out a hand to indicate those steers Marti had sent scattering among the trees.

'She was doing her best!' Jessica defended loyally, casting her stepsister an exasperated look.

'But which evidently isn't good enough!' retorted Elizabeth, undeterred.

Since she really couldn't dispute the younger girl's claims, Marti merely started for her own mount which had come to a halt immediately she had left its back, but was then forced to a stop herself on finding Farrell blocking her path with his own chestnut gelding.

'Well?' he probed shortly.

She shrugged, keeping her gaze fixed to the sleek but powerful shoulder confronting her. 'You heard Elizabeth, I lost control.'

'In that case, I suggest you just keep to tailing in future,' he directed in taut accents. 'And preferably with your mind on what you're doing! That way, we might not have to spend the rest of the day re-mustering the same animals all the time!' The parting-shot was delivered in cutting accents as he wheeled the gelding away and set off after the disappearing cattle— with Elizabeth rapidly following him.

Marti watched them go with her lips levelling in disgruntlement. She didn't know why he should apparently have become so annoyed just because she hadn't refuted the dark-haired girl's claims. He hadn't appeared to take the matter so seriously when he'd first arrived on the scene. In fact, he'd been unexpectedly understanding, as she recollected. She expelled a long breath, half hoping that both he and his female shadow would also bite the dust before the day was out.

Behind her, Jessica had already remounted, but

before doing the same Marti took the chance to lengthen her stirrups, as she had earlier planned, then proceeded to climb into the saddle again, very slowly, and smothering a groan as she did so.

'I guess you must be starting to feel tired too, not being used to this sort of thing,' Jessica smiled sympathetically, and evidently assuming that to be the cause of her friend's wooden movements. 'But take heart, I expect we'll be stopping for lunch shortly once this mob's been yarded, and then you'll be able to have a sit and relax for a while.'

Sit! Marti sincerely doubted she would ever voluntarily sit again in her life. 'Well, I won't deny I'll certainly appreciate the rest,' was all she said aloud. Even if it did mean standing the whole time, it would be a blessed relief just to be able to leave the back of her horse! A familiar young figure crossed her line of vision as they returned to the rear of the heard, prompting the dry protest, 'But not Elizabeth, Jess, please! I couldn't possibly have ever been quite as objectionable as she is, surely!'

'No, I'll give you that, you were certainly never as bitchy as she can be,' Jessica conceded. A pause. 'And I still hope you don't allow her attitude to ruin your time here. Unfortunately, having lost her own mother when she was only six, she was spoilt dreadfully by Roy over the years in recompense, as it were, so that now she's still finding it difficult to accept that her wishes and thoughts aren't the only ones that count any more.' She sighed. 'Which still wouldn't have been too bad, I suppose, if she hadn't developed this possessive attachment she has for Farrell. I'm just hoping—him too, most likely,' on a wry note, 'that she grows out of it again before too long, and then things may be able to return to normal.'

Marti was beginning to wonder just what did constitute normal with regard to herself, but unwilling to delve too deeply into the subject, elected to change the subject instead.

'And all these cattle?' She pointed to the steadily mounting numbers in front of them. 'Do they really require this many for the rodeo?'

'Oh, no!' Jessica shook her head. 'Once they're in the yards up ahead they'll all be drafted, and those not needed will be loaded into the truck—see, it's there already,' gesturing towards a double-decker cattle-trailer waiting beside the yards, 'and taken down to the saleyards at Mareeba, on the Tablelands. The rest we'll walk back to the homestead holding-yards, and then discover if the men out at Iron Pot have been able to come up with anything.' A note of amusement entered her voice.

'Iron Pot?' Marti queried.

'Mmm, it's a mustering-camp way out there.' Jessica indicated a rugged, blue-capped range on the horizon. 'For the most part it's pretty inaccessible country, but I understand they've had a team of men bull-running out there for the last week, and if they have managed to pick up a few scrubbers it could make things just that little bit livelier in the yards.'

Marti nodded, but had little chance to add anything further on the matter for now they were approaching their own yards and the confrontation between two opposing forces began, the cattle stubborn in their reluctance to enter, and the men even more resolute in their determination that they would.

Soon the air was filled with dust as the churning feet of the increasingly vocal animals had it rising in red clouds, but no matter how often they tried to avoid the open gate, or to break away, there was always someone there to force them back again. The noise of cracking whips and barking dogs, along with a sight of horsemen propping and whirling their mounts so expertly, added to the action, and to her amazement Marti felt an entirely unanticipated stirring of excitement within her as she watched what she had to admit, if only to herself, was an extremely vivid and exhilarating scene.

Then suddenly, the last of the gates was swung shut, although the reluctantly penned cattle still continued to mill about in frustrated confusion, a few even demonstrating their anger by charging the rails that enclosed them.

'Come on, let's go and wash some of this dust off, shall we?' Jessica suggested, motioning towards the long trough that ran from the holding-tank beside a tall windmill that pumped the underground water into it. Dismounting, she loosened the girth strap for the horse's comfort in the heat, then haltered it alongside some of the others in the shade of a large tree, and waited patiently until Marti had stiffly followed suit. 'After that, we'll probably have lunch. I expect they brought it out with them in the truck.'

Still in a somewhat bemused state at having discovered something else in the bush that appealed to her—not to mention feeling as if every muscle was bruised and torn—Marti kept up with her as best she could. She didn't want to make it obvious to everyone, especially Farrell and Elizabeth, just how unprepared she had been for this expedition.

'Will we have to help get it ready?' she enquired a trifle apprehensively, remembering Farrell's remarks in that regard during their journey from Cairns, but simultaneously doubting she was in a position to do anything but sag at the moment.

Jessica shook her head and unknowingly gave the reply her companion had been hoping for. 'No, I shouldn't think so. I expect it will be cold meats and salad, and we'll all just help ourselves.' Reaching the trough, which was already being well utilised by some of the men, she found a space for them at one end and began sluicing her face enthusiastically. 'As for the tea, one of the men will probably make that. They usually do.' She grinned. 'When they're in camp, I don't think they like the way we women make it. They prefer it black and strong enough to stand a spoon up in.'

'I know,' lamented Marti, the water running down her own face adding to the mournfulness of her words. 'I don't suppose they might have sent out some milk and sugar from the homestead as well, though, would they?' She eyed the other girl half doubtfully, half hopefully.

Jessica smiled understandingly at her lugubrious expression but had to disappoint her all the same. 'You may be lucky, of course, but I'd really have to say I doubt anyone would have thought of it. They're so accustomed to just sending out the same items all the time, you see.'

Marti nodded, wrinkling her nose in despair.

'And how have you two been doing? We haven't seen much of you this morning,' Vern Stephens's voice suddenly sounded beside her as he and Roy also came to make use of the trough. 'Been enjoying yourselves, have you?'

As enjoyment was actually the last thing she was feeling, Marti made do with a diplomatic, if wry, 'It's certainly been an experience I won't forget.'

'That's good, that's good!' he smiled genially, taking the remark for agreement. 'I'm glad you're finding it interesting. I'm sure Harry will be too when he hears about it. It's a pity he couldn't make it himself, of course, but we're very pleased you could come instead.'

'Thank you, Uncle Vern,' she rejoined sincerely. 'I'm very pleased to be here.' Which might not have been quite genuine, but she thought too much of him to have said otherwise.

'Well, don't let me hold you up,' he urged in the same kindly fashion. 'You go and have some tea and something to eat. You too, young Jess. I've no doubt you're both longing for something to get the dust out of your throats.'

Making suitable replies, the two girls did as suggested, helping themselves to some meat and salad, which Marti made into a sandwich so that she could eat it while standing, and accepting with differing emotions their mugs of tea from the ringer who poured it for them, Jessica with pleasure, being used to such fare, and Marti resignedly, because there wasn't any choice.

But when her friend found a place beside her brother and some of the other men to sit and eat her lunch, Marti made the excuse of wanting to look over the yards in order not to do the same. She was positive that her aching legs would never permit her to bend to such a degree without bringing forth tell-tale groans, or that even if they did, rising upright again later would present even greater problems.

As it was, her perambulations were conducted at a snail's pace, her consumption of her tea still slower. Nevertheless, although probably no less strong than that which Farrell had first made, she was at least able to drink it, most likely because she was so thirsty she felt she could have drunk anything, or . . . could she possibly have been becoming used to the damned stuff? she wondered sardonically.

Leaning against the loading-ramp attached to the yards for a while, Marti glanced casually at the bush surrounding them, her ears gradually becoming attuned to its drowsy stillness, broken only by the occasional rustle of leaves as a faint breath of moving air disturbed them. Abruptly, she caught sight of a flock of red-collared lorikeets, their royal-blue heads, bright-green wings, and red-and-yellow undersides making a glorious splash of colour against the cloudless, azure sky as they winged their chattering way over the yards and into the trees beyond.

'Now tell me you see better than that in the city.' Farrell's expressively drawling voice close by her ear had her jumping a little at his unnoticed approach.

Marti didn't pretend not to know what he was referring to, but grudgingly conceding he could have been right, and admitting it—to him, especially—were two different things. 'Neon lights come in pretty colours too,' she shrugged.

He took an audible breath, the lines of his mouth tightening. 'And naturally your biased belief that whatever the city has to offer is automatically superior to anything in the country extends to people as well! Is that why you've made such an effort to distance yourself from everyone here? Because you consider them beneath you?' he grated contemptuously.

Marti blinked rapidly. That such a construction might have been put upon her action in not joining the others had never occurred to her, but even so something held her back from hotly denying the contention, probably a streak of perverseness brought about by his infuriating condemnations of both herself and her chosen way of life, she surmised.

'If that's what you wish to think,' she allowed with another negligent hunching of a slender shoulder.

Farrell's eyes snapped with an ominous look. 'What I think, I believe I'd better keep to myself, or the fur might really start to fly!' he declared expressively and, turning on his heel, began striding back towards the others swiftly, barely suppressed anger evident in every forceful step.

Marti watched his departure with her lips caught between her teeth, wondering why she should be feeling so dissatisfied with the results her comments had produced. What did it matter to her how he thought of her? Expelling a heavy breath, she resumed her ambling inspection of the yards, hoping the exercise might help reduce the effects of the afternoon's riding yet to come.

Whether they did or not, Marti wasn't really able to tell, because by the time the mustering party finally returned to the homestead just as the sun was sinking below the tops of the trees, she doubted whether she could have felt more stiff and sore if she hadn't been out of the saddle at all. And to think she had considered one night spent sleeping on the ground had made her muscles ache, she recalled with hollow humour. It appeared a positive featherbed to her now!

'Well, it seems the fellers from the Iron Pot did bring in a few scrubbers, after all,' Jessica remarked as they unsaddled their mounts, and nodding towards some wild-eyed, hump-backed bullocks, their great heads surmounted by long, wicked-looking horns, that occupied a separate yard of their own. 'Shall we go down and have a closer look after we've finished here?'

Only just managing to drag the saddle from the back of the grey she had been riding, Marti made one last valient effort and threw it over the rail of the paddock they were in, then shook her head wearily. 'You can if you like, but if you don't mind, I think I'll just head for the house and, hopefully, a long, hot bath.'

'Oh, of course, I should have realised,' the other girl immediately smiled apologetically. 'You're probably tired, and maybe even bruised a little after your fall. You go on up to the homestead, then, and have a bit of a rest, and I'll see you later.'

'Okay.' Marti was only too thankful to agree, and set off slowly for the house. The rest of them, she noticed, all seeming to be making for the bullocks' pen.

An hour or so later, after a long soak and a change of clothes, Marti lay on her bed feeling considerably cleaner but, to her disappointment, only a little less tired and aching. In fact, she had been most surprised to discover that she was only sore, and not raw, as she had quite expected.

Not that it made much difference to how she felt overall, however, so that when Jessica put in an appearance to see if she was coming for a drink before dinner, she gave a shake of her head.

'No, I don't think so, thanks, Jess,' she declined. 'And I'd be grateful if you'd tell Aunt Roma that I'd rather skip dinner tonight as well, if she has no objections.' She gave a disguising half-smile. 'After so many crack-of-the dawn rises the last couple of days, I think I'll just get a very early night.' There was a slight hesitation as her friend nodded her acknowledgement and turned to leave, then, 'Er—before you go, though, I don't suppose you'd have any—umm—liniment, or something similiar, would you?'

'So you did get some bruises in that fall,' Jessica smiled ruefully. 'I'll see what I can do for you. I haven't got any with me, but I'm sure Roma will have some around somewhere.'

Alone once more, Marti struggled to her feet and padded on bare feet to the chest of drawers set against the opposite wall and extracted her nightdress. If she changed now it would just save that much time later. She had only just undone the top two buttons of her silk blouse, though, when there was a cursory knock on her door and Farrell paced—stormed, more like—into the room without waiting for any invitation, slamming the door shut behind him.

Dressed now in hip-moulding pants and a dark-blue-knit shirt, his dark hair tending to curl damply, his bronzed skin exuding a faintly spicy tang of aftershave, his undeniable vitality seemed a direct assault on her own wilted state, and magnified it accordingly.

'Okay, so what are you up to this time, Marti?' he demanded grimly.

She stared at him blankly, quite forgetting to complain about his entering her room without permission. 'Meaning?'

'Meaning, a few bruises,' he tossed a bottle containing some white lotion on to her bed, 'and you suddenly want to miss dinner! Is it all becoming too much for you?' His mockery had a biting edge to it.

Under normal circumstances, she would have retaliated in kind. But not at the moment, not after the revelations she had been forced to acknowledge the last couple of days, not while she was feeling so vulnerable and his physical presence was so dominant that it seemed to fill the whole room.

'N-no,' she faltered. 'I just felt tired and—and . . .'

'Wanted to be alone again so you could wallow in more self-pity, is that it?'

'You consider I have cause to, then?' She tried a dismal gibe in desperation.

'No, but if you're short on reasons, maybe *this* will help!' Jerking her into his arms, his mouth slanted across hers roughly in a long, ravaging kiss that had her gasping and every vestige of weariness abruptly deserted her.

Caught off-guard, Marti stood immobile for a moment as a shock wave of unexpected, and even more unsettling, warmth coursed through her, and then she began fighting as best she could to be free, knowing she had been on the point of responding.

'Get out of here, Farrell! And don't you ever dare do that again!' she railed at him furiously on wrestling herself from his hold.

To her escalating vexation, he merely tapped her provokingly beneath the chin. 'Well, at least it succeeded in getting you firing on all four again,' he drawled lazily. 'You've been very withdrawn since yesterday, and I think I prefer you fiery. That way I've got a better idea of what you're thinking.' His mouth curved into a chafing smile that had her eyes flashing green sparks.

And to think she had nearly responded to what had been a mere ruse! 'You reptile!' she burst out infuriatedly, aiming a flying hand at the side of his deeply tanned face with all her weight behind it.

Arrested before it could reach its mark, the ensuing sudden halt to her momentum sent a jarring shudder racing down her spine, which had her uttering an involuntary cry of pain and clenching her teeth until the spasm slowly receded.

'What the hell?' Farrell caught her by the shoulders, frowning down at her strained features. 'Did you damn well injure yourself in that fall, after all?' he rasped angrily.

'N-not really.' She swallowed hard. 'And—and I'm

sorry I cried out like that. I didn't mean to.'

'That has nothing to do with it!' He waved aside her apology peremptorily. 'What I want to know is, *why*?'

Marti chewed at her lip, debating whether she could fob him off with an excuse, and then, surmising he was too astute, and persistent, to fall for anything she could come up with on the spur of the moment, drew a deep breath and disclosed on a somewhat defiant note, 'It's been a long time since I last went riding!'

Farrell's eyes widened in sudden comprehension. 'You mean, you allowed yourself to get *saddle-sore* to that extent? Of all the bloody senseless, stubborn, asinine . . .!' he castigated exasperatedly. 'Why in blazes didn't you say something? You could at least have saved yourself some discomfort by returning in the truck instead of riding back!' Catching hold of her chin, he tilted it upwards inexorably. 'Or would that have been too much like admitting you weren't superior to everyone else here?'

'It's only you who think I see myself that way!' she threw back, smarting under his denunciations. 'Because, if you must know, it was probably more a case of the shoe being on the other foot! *I* didn't want to appear inferior to everyone else!' Resentment had her revealing more than she had intended, and she pulled away from him vexedly, flushing slightly.

'And that would have been just too unbearable to accept, apparently!' he said sarcastically.

'With Elizabeth just sweating on any opportunity to be disparaging, yes, it was!' she retorted huffily.

'You're saying, you let yourself be pushed into this state by some adolescent's childishly gibing comments?' Farrell gave an incredulous shake of his head. 'Give me strength! I would never have believed it!

Someone ought to towel your backside good and proper for being as irrationally infantile as she is!'

Having already berated herself soundly for permitting Elizabeth's remarks to goad her into even joining the muster in the first place, Marti really found herself unable to rebuff his condemnation. In lieu, with her sense of humour unexpectedly surfacing, just as it had the day before, she settled for a partly self-mocking, partly rueful, 'Although not right at the moment, I trust,' in response to his latter proposal.

A slow smile touched the corners of his firm mouth, his thick-lashed eyes crinkling, and incomprehensibly making Marti's heart start thudding against her ribs. 'No, I guess not,' he granted on an indolent note. 'But unless you're figuring on remaining in the same condition indefinitely, I suggest we get on and give nature a hand in repairing the damage.' He bent to pick up the bottle from the bed.

'We?' she queried in dubious surprise.

'Since we're the only two here, and you obviously can't reach your back . . .' He shrugged, and flicked a finger to indicate her blouse. 'I suggest you remove that, and let me get to work.'

Him! 'Oh, but—but there's really no need for you to bother,' she demurred swiftly, backing away a little. 'I'm sure I'll be able to manage.'

'From what I've seen so far, I doubt it.' Impervious, he began removing the cap from the bottle.

Under the circumstances, how could she dispute it? 'Well, even so, I expect Jess . . .'

'Apart from the fact that she's probably having dinner by now, you had your chance to ask Jessica, when you were busily claiming you only had a few bruises,' Farrell cut her off in shortening tones. 'So for God's sake, just stop playing coy, huh? I can assure you I have seen a number of unclothed females before today, so I'm unlikely to lose all semblance of control at the mere sight of some exposed flesh, however shapely.' An element of corrosive mockery made its appearance. 'Particularly, I might add, when what you're no doubt wearing underneath probably covers you better than anything you wear for swimming!'

'Except that, right at present, I don't happen to *be* wearing anything underneath!' Marti flared.

This disclosure had his lips twitching expressively. 'In that case, I suggest you simply clutch something to you appropriately—here, this should do,' tossing her the nightdress she had laid on the bed earlier, 'before I'm tempted to divest you of the other myself, in order to save wasting any more time.'

Although wryly imparted, Marti still had few reservations about his capability of doing as threatened without a second thought, or his likelihood of departing without applying the liniment, and as a result she reasoned she had little option but to acquiesce—albeit grudgingly. When all was said and done, her back *did* feel in dire need of attention.

'Well, turn around, then!' she ordered irritably. 'I've no intention of removing anything with you looking on!'

Farrell inclined his head, more mocking than acknowledging, but did at least turn to face the door, even if with a leisureliness she found aggravating in the extreme. A few moments later, her blouse hastily discarded in favour of the nightdress held tightly to her chest, Marti made certain it was the satin-smooth sweep of her back that was presented to him when she advised he could turn back again.

'Well, it will help if you stand still,' was his first drily voiced remark as he brushed her hair forward from the nape of her neck.

'Sorry,' she mumbled self-consciously, his touch having brought about an involuntary, restless movement of her feet, and did her utmost to ensure no more such betraying displays of nervous awareness occurred.

Starting with her neck and shoulders, Farrell not only rubbed the balm into her skin methodically, but his fingers also lingered to massage those incredibly tightened muscles he appeared to know instinctively required kneading. The effect was what Marti could only have called an exquisite pain—a mixture of agony at having the muscles manipulated, and pleasure at actually being able to feel them loosening under the pressure. That she was also becoming disturbingly conscious of an undeniable enjoyment at the feel of his hands moving over her skin, and not simply for the relief they were providing, she tried to ignore completely.

'I guess that about does it,' Farrell declared finally after having worked his way down to her waist. 'You should be able to manage the rest.' He paused, a rakish grin forming that, in her already distracted state, had Marti's breath catching in her throat. 'However, I've no objections to—er—continuing further, should you . . .'

'No, I don't think so, thank you all the same,' she inserted rapidly, but in much the same whimsical manner, refusing to be provoked into losing her composure totally after what he'd done for her. Her back really did feel considerably better already. 'Although I am grateful for your time and effort, of course.' She hesitated, eyeing him diffidently. 'You would appear to have quite a knack for uncovering just which spots need the most attention.'

His mouth sloped crookedly as he re-capped the

bottle and stood it on the dressing-table. 'Horses, dogs, humans, they all get muscle problems from time to time, and after a while you learn to recognise the troublesome ones by touch,' he relayed in a drawl.

'Oh!' acknowledged Marti lamely, unsure whether she liked being compared to a horse or a dog.

'Though, I must confess, I've never worked on quite such a—umm—curvaceous and silken-skinned creature before,' Farrell added lazily, his gaze expressive as it roamed idly over her.

Abruptly reminded of her lack of apparel, Marti coloured warmly and half turned away to hide her disconcertion. 'Yes—well—as you said, I'm sure I'll be able to manage to rest on my own,' she said as steadily as possible. 'And—and you must be hungry, so don't let me keep you from your own dinner any longer. I've taken up enough of your time, as it is.'

'So you have,' he averred, drily, the reason for such a nuance one that Marti could only frown over perplexedly. He tipped her face up to his briefly as he passed on his way to the door. 'But then, I guess I'll manage to survive.'

Marti didn't doubt he would too. That air of self-reliance, of individualism, about him denoted him as nothing if not a survivor. But with his departure came less easily rationalised thoughts.

First and foremost was the knowledge that on a number of occasions now he had managed to arouse in her emotions she had no business feeling where he was concerned, didn't want to feel, in fact. Oh, he was certainly good-looking enough—hadn't she already admitted that when she first saw him at the airport?—and that air of essential maleness about him could be incontestably stirring too, but that was still no reason for the effect he had on her at times, surely? After all, hadn't she met other men with similar qualities before, and been completely unmoved by them?

Just what made Farrell different, she had no idea, but as she climbed into bed some time later it was with the resolve to be on her guard in future. Good Lord, she didn't want to be attracted to a grazier, of all people, especially not one who was as indelibly a part of the bush as she was of the city. They had absolutely nothing in common—interests, lifestyle, nothing. Why, most times they couldn't even conduct a conversation for more than a few minutes before it degenerated into an argument.

No, she definitely did not need the problems of being attracted, and thereby vulnerable, to anyone from outside her own circle, Marti decided firmly as she prepared for sleep. Her last thought before drifting off—recalling with marked satisfaction Farrell's description of Elizabeth as adolescent and childish—was not quite so supportive, however, particularly when, and much to her exasperation, it promptly engendered a feeling of considerable dissatisfaction on remembering he had declared her to be equally irrational and infantile.

CHAPTER SIX

NEXT morning, Friday, Marti awoke still feeling stiff, but thankfully noticeably less sore. Once breakfast was concluded—at the same unholy hour as the day previous, she noted ruefully—the men immediately disappeared down to the yards in order to draft the cattle and horses into their various pens ready for the weekend's events. For their part, the women all remained in the homestead, including Elizabeth at her stepmother's insistence, to begin their preparations for catering for the anticipated influx of people.

For Marti the day was another filled with new experiences, and despite her determination to remain removed from it all, she soon found it was almost impossible not to become at least a little infected with the same feeling of enjoyable excitement that began to pervade the whole station as the supply truck rattled in and was unloaded of its seemingly mountainous amounts of food and drink; families from surrounding properties arrived to help with the preparations; and later in the day competitors started arriving and setting up camp around the homestead.

By sundown there were something like forty extra vehicles parked about the clearing, and as camp-fires began to flicker into life and people wandered from one fire to another—sharing drinks, swapping yarns, renewing friendships with those they might not have seen since the rodeo the year before—the scene soon took on a carnival atmosphere.

Eventually, it became quieter, though—except for

the occasional bellowing of cattle, the neighing of horses, and the more persistent calls of the coo-ee birds overhead—as fires were doused, the homestead generators were turned off, and everyone settled down to sleep. With space at a premium, Marti now shared Jessica and Elizabeth's room with them, every other bedroom in the house also containing as many occupants as possible, the verandahs strewn with numerous camp beds.

Not that the darkness halted the arrival of more competitors, Marti discovered, for she was awakened a number of times throughout the night by the unexpected rumble of vehicles or the sudden flash of headlights brightening the room briefly. Nevertheless, she still wasn't quite prepared for the sight that met her eyes the next morning, because now she estimated there must have been more than a hundred assorted vehicles reaching down towards the airstrip, with still more arriving as she watched.

With everyone rising at the same time, it immediately became a matter of eating in relays so far as those in the homestead were concerned. From then on it would be a case of *someone* wanting something to eat all the time—the women all sharing the duties of doing the cooking and serving the food—for although most of the camped family groups had brought along their own supplies to cook over the open fires, that didn't apply in the case of the single men who comprised the majority of those present.

Now Marti began to understand the reason for the four to five hundred sausages, the more than one thousand meat pies, the one hundred and fifty loaves of bread, that the supply truck had delivered, not to mention the three hundred and fifty dozen cans of beer and the almost two hundred bottles of soft drink.

The proceeds from the sale of all this food and drink would hopefully provide five to six thousand dollars for the Royal Flying Doctor Service, Roma informed her.

By eight, the first heats of the camp-draft were already under way, and Marti was surprised to see Farrell shortly thereafter make an unexpected entrance into the kitchen where yet another pile of dishes and cutlery was being loaded into the dishwasher. Since learning that he and Braden, along with their father, usually ran the camp-drafting events, she had been anticipating another day free of his company. That his gaze should have promptly singled her out did little to alleviate her sudden feelings of trepidation.

'Come on, you'd better come and watch,' he declared calmly, and encircling her wrist with his fingers headed for the door again with her in tow.

Marti's indignation sky-rocketed, but in view of there being others present, she did her best to keep it from showing as she cast about frantically for an excuse. 'Oh, but—but there's so much help required here,' she protested, hanging back as much as she could, and abruptly finding the prospect of remaining in the kitchen all day markedly more inviting than she had done previously. 'Besides, I'm not all that . . .'

'No, you go along and watch, dear,' Roma Stephens cut in on her with misplaced helpfulness. 'You're a guest, and it is your first visit for the rodeo, when all's said and done. So don't you worry about things here, we'll manage.' She smiled encouragingly.

'Not that she'd be much of a help, anyway. She can't even cook!' was Elizabeth's disparaging contribution, earning her a censuring look from Lucy.

'Can't you?' Farrell quirked a dark brow wryly as,

having been deprived of her excuse, Marti now grudgingly accompanied him down the steps.

'No!' she had no compunction in confirming with something of a snap, her expression defiant. 'And what's more, I'd be grateful if you would stop grabbing hold of my arm all the time!' She struck out wildly at the hand still restraining her. 'I'm not even particularly interested in seeing what's going on down there, in any case!' Flinging out her free hand to denote the large, spectator-crowded yard they were approaching.

'You think I needed to be told that!' The words were ground out harshly, his own demeanour altering now as he brought them to a sudden standstill, his eyes scourging her with a scathing gaze. 'But since it's your own father who always provides the trophy for the event, this year being no exception, the least you can damn well do is watch! And that applies whether you want to or not, you disobliging, inconsiderate, miserable excuse for a daughter!' he flayed unmercifully, jerking them into motion once more. 'Got it?'

With her cheeks burning as much as her temper, Marti had no choice but to struggle to keep up with his forceful, long-legged strides, while within conflicting emotions warred. Outraged though she was that he should have dared to speak to her in such a manner, there was also dismay at the thought that, once again, he had simply succeeded in confronting her with the truth. Over the years she hadn't always been the best of daughters! It was so distressing an idea that it had uncontrollable tears gathering at the back of her eyes, and her outrage died a defeated death.

Leading her around the side of the yard in use, the surrounding top rails of which were packed with

jeans-clad spectators, both male and female, Farrell
eventually brought them to a small stand that
overlooked the arena, which was already occupied by
his father, equipped with a stopwatch and a clipboard
filled with papers, and Roy, armed with a loudspeaker.

Without uttering a word, Farrell urged her up the
few steps, only releasing his grip on her wrist when
she was stationed between himself and his father, and
not between the two older men as she had initially
made to do. Just so he could ensure her attention
didn't wander, she supposed despondently.

'You look flushed, young Marti,' Vern Stephens
smiled down at her as they waited for advice that the
next competitor was ready.

'Mmm, she was in a hurry to get here, in case she
missed any of the action,' put in Farrell on a sardonic
note Marti suspected only she could distinguish.

'Well, you shouldn't be disappointed. We've had
some good rides so far,' the older man said, evidently
accepting his son's words at face value.

Marti nodded, forcing a weak half-smile on to her
lips, although not quite looking at him, and then
turned her face to the yard in front of them quickly.
With her eyes still wet with tears, she didn't want to
generate any questions she would rather not have to
answer at the moment.

Beside her, Farrell bent to rest his tanned and
muscular forearms on the front rail, it being
impossible for her not to be aware of every movement
his powerful body made in such a cramped area, a
circumstance that had her pressing nearer to his father
in the hope of creating some extra space between them.

Leaning forward as he was, however, his head was
on much the same level as her own, and this enabled
him to look into her face despite her trying to keep it

averted. An irritably expelled breath did have her glancing instinctively in his direction a short time later, though. Within their damp frames, her eyes were deep, luminous emerald pools of bitter despair as they connected briefly with his unwavering gaze before she snatched them away again.

'Oh, for God's sake, go then, if it's all so damned repugnant to you!' he rasped savagely under cover of Vern and Roy calling down to Braden in one of the smaller yards next to the stand.

'No, now that I've been dragged here, I'll stay!' she gritted vehemently. 'Until bloody midnight, if necessary!' She wasn't in any mood to mince her own words either. How was she supposed to have known her father donated the trophy for the event? No one had been disposed to inform her of that fact until now! 'While as for you,' she continued, seemingly unable to stop now that she had started, 'get stood on, Farrell!' She swung her gaze back to the yard with a barely audible, choked sob.

He muttered something violent under his breath. 'Then stop being so damned perverse, and go!'

'No, I said I'd stay, and I will!' she said fiercely.

And stay she resolutely did, at first gazing down on the colourful scene spread below her with uncaring and even unseeing eyes on occasion, as the blazing sun beat down from the brilliant, cloudless blue sky above. Then gradually, as the morning progressed, she watched with a faint but ungovernable stirring of interest.

With still more vehicles continuing to arrive, and the intermittent but distinctive drone of engines overhead signifying many had chosen to fly in by light plane as well, the crowd lining the rails was increasing appreciably, and Marti found herself beginning to take it all in curiously, noting the easy camaraderie of the solidly built, sun-darkened men as they watched knowledgeably and judged the ability of each competitor, often with bantering shouts of advice or good humoured roasting, their broad-brimmed, well-worn bush-hats pulled low to keep the sun from their eyes.

Although there were considerably fewer of them, and they weren't anywhere near as vocal, the females among them watched the proceedings just as intently, or at least the younger ones did. The older women obviously preferred to indulge in more leisurely conversation, and to keep an eye on their exuberant offspring.

Over all a fine film of ever-present red dust hung in the hot, dry air, stirred up by not only the pounding hoofs of the animals but by hundreds of booted feet also, which at times lent the setting an almost mystic quality that Marti found strangely picturesque. Not that she indicated by so much as a word or a look that she approved of anything she saw, regardless.

When proceedings halted for lunch, Marti purchased hers willingly—she certainly had no objections to supporting such a good cause—but then wandered back to the stand to eat it alone. She felt—not to put too fine a point on it—something of a misfit, she decided as she chewed her way through her steakburger contemplatively.

It wasn't a feeling she had ever experienced before, and not only was it one she didn't like, she also suspected that, subconsciously at least, she wished she weren't quite so much the outsider. An unthinkable desire a week ago, she conceded wryly, and not one she was likely to achieve either by eating alone, she supposed. But after her last confrontation with Farrell she had really felt the need for some solitude in order both to re-gather her thoughts and to recover her equilibrium.

'What on earth are you doing here? Sulking?' A pause. 'Or didn't you want to miss the opportunity of wishing me good luck?'

It seemed just to think about him made him appear, grimaced Marti, on looking to her left and discovering Farrell only a yard or so away, the horse he had ridden the day before saddled and standing quietly beside him, ready for their approaching time to compete.

'Neither!' she replied to both his questions with something of a snap. It was all right for him to revert to being sardonic! *He* hadn't had to suffer his deprecatory tongue-lashing. 'I was merely enjoying the respite!' She sent him a pointed glance as she rose to her feet and, turning her back on him, tossed her rubbish into a nearby empty fuel-drum which had been provided for just such a purpose, and marched up the stairs to the top platform. Others were starting to return to the yard now as well, she noted.

'While dreaming of all the delights of the city you would rather be encountering, huh?'

'What else?' she wasn't above retorting, keeping her back to him. Far be it from her to give him the satisfaction of knowing it had almost been the reverse.

Farrell made an indeterminate sound—exasperation or resignation? She couldn't decide which—but when the expected ensuing retort didn't come, she chanced a swift look over her shoulder, and discovered him to have moved on to one of the smaller yards where he was now conversing with Braden and Trent. With a shrug she determinedly expelled him from her thoughts, and gave a welcoming smile to Vern and Roy as they rejoined her in the stand.

The skilful exhibition of riding and anticipation Marti presently watched Farrell give in the ring wasn't able to be disregarded quite so easily, though, she found. For it was purely finely honed co-ordination and ability that enabled him to complete his round without an error, and in by far the fastest time yet recorded, and it was impossible for her to deny that it had absorbed her interest entirely.

Nor was she really at all surprised when no one, male or female—not even Jessica or Elizabeth, who both proved to be extremely proficient—managed to better his time so that at the end of the competition he was duly declared the winner, amid much clapping, raillery, and general conviviality. Although the presentation that followed was a part of the proceedings definitely not to her liking, when she realised it had been taken for granted that she would do the honours on her father's behalf.

Worse, she despaired on observing the second and third place-getters being awarded their prizes, by Alison and Jessica as it so happened, when they received a kiss as well for their efforts. Consequently, when it was her turn to approach Farrell in the dusty arena, it was with some reluctance that she handed him the small cup, mumbled something appropriate for such an occasion, and stretched upwards to bestow the obligatory peck on his cheek.

Still mounted, as had been the other two, Farrell bent low, but instead of simply offering his lean, bronzed cheek, he swept her closer with his free arm, and before she could guess what he intended his lips took possession of hers in a leisurely, compelling kiss that had her mouth waywardly parting in response even as she strained to be free.

'You'd better smile, the old man's got his camera

out,' he drawled tauntingly on finally releasing her and straightening, to the accompaniment of much whistling and good-natured cheering from those lining the yard.

Bright colour stained Marti's cheeks and her eyes sparked green fire as she glared up at him balefully, but with a superhuman effort she did manage to force her lips into a semblance of a smile—for appearances' sake; not that she permitted that to stop her from promptly denouncing him succinctly between her teeth: 'Bastard!'

Farrell flicked a brow goadingly high. 'For eliciting a response?'

'For being your contemptible, hateful self!' she hissed, only just remembering to retain her fixed smile as she turned on her heel and made for the gate leading out of the yard.

From behind her came a low, warm laugh, a delightfully husky sound that, despite her simmering feelings, still managed to unsettle Marti's senses, and as a result had her berating herself for being all manner of fools on her storming walk back to the homestead.

That evening there was to be a barbecue and dance, and the three girls made the best they could of their somewhat crowded quarters as they made ready for it. Elizabeth still couldn't restrain herself from making another of her venomous comments prior to leaving the room.

'That's a bit swish, isn't it?' she scorned on seeing the very elegant though simply designed dress of checked Thai silk Marti had chosen to wear. 'Who are you hoping to impress? Farrell?' Her brown eyes narrowed with suspicion.

The assumption was so wide of the mark that Marti uttered an ironical laugh, which thankfully helped her retain her control, because she really wasn't inclined to accept any more darts being thrown in her direction that day. 'Not at all,' she shrugged. 'It was merely less up-market than any of the others I'd brought with me.'

'Oh, pardon me!' quipped Elizabeth sarcastically, dropping a mock-curtsey. 'I'd forgotten we had one of the *beautiful people* deigning to visit us!'

'That's quite all right,' Marti allowed with equally feigned sweetness, her patience rapidly deteriorating. 'Because I'm sure you'll manage to put us all in the shade. Your own dress suits you so well and is quite charming. I had one very much the same when I was at school.'

The younger girl's antagonistic expression was immediately supplanted by one of wide-eyed dismay as she glanced down at the garment that had just been downgraded to childish and out-of-date.

Jessica, meanwhile, gave a rueful shake of her head. 'You deserved that, Liz!' she half laughed. 'I could have told you, Marti's always been able to deliver a good set-down if she felt it was needed.'

Except where one arrogant, censuring, and totally provoking male was concerned, apparently, mused Marti expressively.

'But—but . . . my dress!' Elizabeth wailed, evidently uncaring of whether the remark had been deserved or not at the moment. 'I didn't bring another one with me!'

'Oh, for heaven's sake, there's nothing wrong with the one you've got on!' her stepsister exclaimed on a partly exasperated, partly wry note. 'Marti only said what she did in order to shut you up.' An amused curve shaped her mouth. 'And it would appear she succeeded most admirably.'

'You mean, it's not really out-of-date?' the dark-haired girl enquired of Marti, albeit a trifle dubiously.

Already regretting having let herself be goaded into something by Elizabeth once again, as well as remembering just how easily one's confidence could be shattered at seventeen, Marti smiled and gave a negative shake of her head.

'Oh, I'm so pleased!' Elizabeth heaved a sigh of relief. Then, after a slight hesitation, she hurried on to apologise. 'I'm sorry for what I said about yours.' She bit at her lip contritely. 'I was probably only jealous because it looks so nice and the colours are so pretty.'

'Although it *is* a bit swish for a barbecue,' Marti acceded humorously, doing her bit to smooth over the situation.

The other girl pulled an eloquent face. 'With looks like yours, who's going to notice what you're wearing?' And as if embarrassed by having admitted as much, she followed with a quick, 'I'll see you later, then,' and departed.

'Well, well, from enemy to fan in one quick reversal,' Jessica quipped.

It was a pity she couldn't achieve the same results with Farrell, Marti suddenly found herself thinking, and promptly pulled herself up short. Was she mad? She didn't want him interested in her any more than she wanted to be interested in him.

'Yes—well—I'd certainly rather be on friendly terms with her,' she conceded, walking to the door herself now. 'So if you're ready, shall we make for the barbecue as well?'

'May as well,' Jessica agreed equably, and together they made their way down to the area set aside for the evening's entertainment.

With the men from the homestead, together with those on the organising committee, taking over the task of cooking the mounds of steak, chops, and other accompaniments, which kept them busy for some considerable time until everyone's appetite had been finally satisfied, their womenfolk made the most of the opportunity to relax and eat a leisurely meal, Marti and Jessica among them.

Not that either of them was permitted to remain without male company for long, anyway, for with Wayne Carberry, the young station-manager who had caught Jessica's interest otherwise engaged in helping with the cooking, and Marti not having a partner in any case, they were both looked upon as unattached females. With so many single males present, and relatively few unmarried girls, there weren't many moments when either of them wasn't surrounded by a number of lean, bronzed, young men.

It was yet another entirely new experience for Marti—not that she had ever lacked for partners among her own set in Brisbane—but this was completely different, and certainly something to raise the morale of someone whose self-esteem had taken quite a battering during the preceding few days. The effect was that she began to relax and enter into the spirit of things as she never had done previously, the more so after consuming a couple of glasses of wine someone produced just before the dancing began.

It also enabled her to react more naturally when Farrell eventually claimed her for a dance some time later in the evening.

'Well, don't tell me you've actually found something to smile about,' he drawled in wryly disbelieving tones as he began leading her competently to the strains of the music coming from the tape-recorder, his eyes ranging slowly over her glowing face. 'Or does it just remind you of similar affairs elsewhere?'

'Oh, no, I've never attended anything quite like this before,' she smiled spontaneously, her even white teeth shining. 'This is a first in every sense.'

'But an agreeable one for a change, hmm?'

Marti nodded, discovering she liked being held in his arms and feeling his strong muscles flex as they moved. She cast him a glance from beneath long, curling lashes. 'Is that so unbelievable?'

'You're asking *me* that?' A dark brow crooked eloquently.

He was right, of course. She hadn't anticipated finding anything pleasant about her visit, or anything to interest her. 'Well, if you weren't always so ready to find fault with me all the time,' she parried, shrugging.

'You mean, in the same way you're unbiased about everything associated with the bush?' he asked drily. His eyes took on a lazy look. 'Besides, I don't recall faulting you at the presentation this afternoon, and look at the reception that received.'

Twin spots of colour appeared in Marti's cheeks at the recollection, and momentarily she dropped her gaze. Was he meaning while he had been kissing her, or afterwards? On lifting her eyes again, she held his gaze tenaciously. 'Because it was done solely to annoy,' she contended with assumed lightness, refusing to let him unsettle her.

Farrell's lips twitched, but he didn't comment, only going on to quiz, 'So will you be watching the rodeo events tomorrow too?'

'Why, does my father donate trophies for some of those as well?' she countered wryly.

'Only one,' he advised, his mouth curving engagingly.

'Then I guess it's my bounden duty to watch, isn't it?'

His eyes surveyed her animated face meditatively. 'You don't have to, if you don't want to.'

'You mean, you're actually giving me the choice?' she bantered. 'Well, just fancy that! You really think I can be relied upon to make the right decision?' The faintest hint of mockery edged into her voice.

'Since the only occasion on which you did actually make a decision resulted in your hardly being able to walk that could be a debatable point,' he was quick to taunt in return. A captivating tilt caught at one corner of his well-shaped mouth. 'So how are all the aches and pains, anyway?'

'Oh, just about gone now,' Marti was glad to be able to report, and even more pleased for the chance to avoid responding to that first somewhat pertinent remark.

'You won't be wanting another rub-down, then?'

'Are you offering?'

For a second or two Farrell's darkening hazel eyes delved deeply into lively emerald, his arms tightening about her fractionally. Then he gave a rueful shake of his head. 'You're tipsy! he charged in dry tones.

'No, I'm not,' she denied with a slightly shaky laugh. That look in his eyes had tautened every nerve and electrified her senses. 'I've had a couple of glasses of wine, I admit, but . . .' She came to an abrupt halt as a furious bellow suddenly rent the air, shortly followed by an increasing number of somewhat more agitated than irate ones, and she turned her head in the direction of the yards, as did everyone else.

Farrell uttered a stifled oath, releasing Marti immediately, and inclining his head in a gesture of regret. 'Sorry, sweetheart, but it would appear it's *my* duty calling at the moment. I thought we might get trouble with one particular bull the men brought in, and at a guess I'd say that's what's happened.' He flashed her a grin as he began moving. 'Perhaps two nights' captivity was all he was prepared to stand.'

Well, at least there was no lack of experienced men able and willing to help rectify whatever was wrong, Marti mused humorously on observing the swift exodus to the yards of just about every male on the scene.

From beside the barbecue area Jessica beckoned her to join her. 'I'm going to go down and have a look at what's going on,' she said immediately on Marti's arrival. 'Do you want to come too?'

Marti hesitated, then nodded as she saw a number of other girls already heading in that direction. 'In view of the numbers already there, do you think we'll be able to get close enough actually to see anything?' she half laughed as they began following the rest. 'Not that there seems much light to see by, in any case.'

'Oh, it only appears that way because we've just left the homestead lights,' her friend brushed aside the comment matter-of-factly. She glanced up at the sky, studded with myriad stars. 'There's a full moon, though, so we should be able to see pretty well.'

And much to Marti's surprise, she found they could, once their eyes had adjusted to the change, although for a time, as they searched for a vantage point, that still didn't allow them to discover just exactly what had occurred, or was now occuring. They could hear a number of directions being given, and see a lot of movement, but until they decided to climb—somewhat awkwardly due to their attire—to the top rail of one of the nearby pens, their curiosity remained unappeased.

'So that's what happened.' Jessica nodded her

comprehension immediately she could look across to where the men were.

'What?' queried Marti, her inexperienced eyes still unable to distinguish what was taking place even though she was peering in the same direction.

'One of the scrubbers has tried to jump the rails, couldn't quite make it, and has got himself stuck astraddle of it instead.'

Marti gulped, and looked down at the cattle milling below her apprehensively. She didn't realise they jumped—and certainly not that high! 'Do they often do that?'

'Oh, some of them do, especially the wild ones,' Jessica relayed casually. 'Unfortunately, though it can become a rather dicey exercise getting them back on the ground again, without either them or the men suffering injury in the process, when they get themselves caught up in the rails like this one has. Farell reckoned the other day that this one—at least, I'm fairly sure it's the same one—should have been put in one of the smaller yards. He wouldn't have been able to get such a run at it then. He would have to have been satisfied with just charging.' She gave a graphic half-laugh.

That didn't sound all that much better to Marti. 'He's not one of the ones they'll be using tomorrow, though?'

Jessica shook her head. 'No, scrubbers can be used, but usually it's more convenient not to. It can be dangerous enough just using open-range cattle—even when everything's conducted all in accordance with the relevant rules and regulations, as this rodeo is—without the extra danger involved in getting them through the yards, not to mention to their eventual riders, of course. Some of these,' pointing to the ones below them, 'can be unpredictable enough once someone gets on their back.'

Marti nodded, eyeing the beasts concerned warily again. 'So what will be done with the—umm—scrubbers?'

'Oh, I think they're destined to be trucked down to the meatworks on Monday for pet food,' the other girl supplied a little vaguely, her attention evidently on what was happening at the other yard. 'There! They've got him down! See?'

'Mmm, I can now.'

'Well, I guess that's our bit of excitement over for the night,' grinned Jessica, already starting to climb back down to the ground. 'I think I'll go and find Wayne. You coming?'

'But there's still something happening over there,' Marti said, continuing to look towards the other yard.

'They're probably just moving him into another pen.'

'Would you mind if I stayed to watch while they do it?' Marti glanced down to ask. 'It doesn't look as if he's all that keen on being moved.'

Jessica laughed. 'No, doubtless he isn't. But you stay, if you want. I'll see you back at the homestead.'

Marti nodded her acknowledgement and, as Jessica began moving away, returned her gaze to the action. She gave an occasional gasp on seeing the bull sweep his long horns between the rails of the alleys among the pens in an effort to reach his captors, her eyes unconsciously seeking one particular male figure amid many.

'Do you come here often?' Farrell's drily humorous enquiry made so close to her a few minutes later startled Marti so much that she almost toppled from her precarious perch. No wonder she hadn't been able to locate him, she mused ironically.

Aloud, she half laughed, half censured, 'Don't do that! I could have fallen in with *them*!' gesturing briefly to the beasts on the other side of the rails.

'Mmm, you do look a trifle perilously balanced,' he agreed. 'Would you like a lift down?'

'No, I can manage,' she demurred, feeling with her foot for the next rail. For some incomprehensible reason, she didn't think she wanted to be that close to him now that most of the others appeared to have returned to the homestead. 'I was just watching until . . .' She broke off with an alarmed intake of breath as her high-heeled shoe slipped on the round steel bar and she felt herself falling—until Farrell's hands caught her on either side of her slender waist, and lowered her more gently.

'Thank you,' she acknowledged gratefully, but taking a couple of hasty steps backward. 'I'm afraid I'm not really wearing the most appropriate attire for climbing.'

He shrugged in a deprecatory manner. 'So what made you come down here in the first place?'

'To see what was happening, naturally! I came with Jess, but she left to find Wayne just before you arrived.'

'While you stayed to watch even longer?' His expression was one of lightly mocking disbelief. 'That surely wouldn't have been a sign of interest, would it?'

Marti slanted him a glance, unknowingly both piquant and provocative, from between the fringes of her glossy lashes. 'And if it was?'

He reached out a hand to trail a solitary finger along the underside of her fragilely moulded jaw. 'Well, was it?' he quizzed softly.

She moistened her lips nervously, her breathing becoming a little ragged as a result of his disturbing touch. What was she doing? she wondered in sudden dismay. Letting the wine she had consumed dictate her behaviour, or merely using it as an excuse in order to do as her senses directed?

'As a matter of fact, yes,' she disclosed in a rush, but on an almost defiant note. About to continue, she felt something hard knock against her back, and suddenly remembering the cattle behind her, as well as the bull slashing its horns between the rails, she immediately gave a gasp of fear and automatically leapt forward, straight into Farrell's arms, for the second time in as many minutes.

When a swift look over her shoulder showed it to have been nothing but an inquisitive cow, and a de-horned one at that, Marti uttered a partly flustered, partly relieved, half-laugh. 'I'm sorry,' she murmured self-consciously, trying to take a step backward but finding his strong arms preventing any such move. 'I—I didn't mean to throw myself at you. I just didn't know what it was.'

'So who's finding fault?' Farrell countered in an indolent drawl, his arms imperceptibly drawing her closer, one hand sliding upwards to brush against the nape of her neck disconcertingly.

Marti swallowed convulsively, and brought her hands up to his broad chest in an effort to keep him at a distance. 'Yes—well—I think it's time we . . .'

'You're so right,' he inserted in a deepening tone as his well defined mouth lowered to capture hers in a long, searing kiss that sent tremors of shockingly intense feeling racing along her every nerve.

For a moment Marti struggled against the com-pelling contact, but the hand cupping her nape nullified her every attempt at resistance relentlessly, and when her own hands, as if of their own accord, traitorously stopped pushing in favour of clasping about the wide expanse of his back, she finally gave up fighting for feeling.

On a tremulous sigh, her lips parted invitingly beneath the consuming pressure of his, her senses beginning to whirl, a fiery blaze of desire overtaking her. Oblivious to everything save the stimulation of powerful arms holding her close to his virile, hard-muscled length, and the demands of his warm, exciting mouth that generated a fervent response impossible to control, she melted against him sinuously.

When he at last raised his head, a faintly self-mocking smile touched Farrell's lips briefly. 'I guess you're just too damned beautiful for your own good, sweetheart . . . and mine,' he murmured expressively.

With her face burning at the thought of her uninhibited response, Marti inhaled deeply in an attempt to steady her breathing and shrugged with forced indifference. 'Yes, well, even antagonists can become—er—carried away at times on such star-spangled, moonlit nights, I suppose,' she just managed to push out excusingly, albeit mainly on her own behalf. She faced him resolutely. 'So shall we return to the homestead now?'

'Perhaps we'd better.' His concurrence was sardonically dry. 'Otherwise, who can tell what reactions continued exposure to such celestial forces might conceivably inspire?'

Thinking it prudent not to attempt to acknowledge the deliberately facetious remark, Marti merely began making for the homestead in as outwardly controlled a manner as possible. Inside, it was a different matter entirely, however, for there she was a mass of confused, conflicting, and churning emotions she didn't really manage to come to grips with until they had all eventually retired for the night.

CHAPTER SEVEN

ALTHOUGH not requiring to be forced into watching the rodeo events the following day, Marti purposely took her time before ambling down to the yards, even so her expression carefully schooled to display an aloof interest only. Having finally admitted to herself that Farrell did hold an attraction for her, and an unexpectedly strong one at that, she had decided that polite but impersonal was the best attitude for her to adopt in future. Since nothing could ever possibly come from such a relationship, what was the point of encouraging it? This had been her determining judgment. No, she would be far better off keeping all her thoughts and feelings strictly to herself.

Consequently, there was no indication on her face whatsoever of the undeniable excitement, or moments of alarm, that Marti felt as each competitor pitted their skills against those of the pawing, bucking, truculent beasts they did battle with. And today the dust really did fly, she noticed, as well as many riders less capable of remaining airborne, although how any of them managed to stay seated for their allotted time in some events she never knew.

Or how those who didn't managed to survive the falls they took either, if it came to that. It was probably their youth—the majority of those contesting the bull-riding and buck-jumping events being in their late teens or early twenties—and the hard, physical, outdoor life they lived which would surely toughen anyone, she surmised eventually.

The steer-wrestling she viewed in considerably less trepidation and, in fact, she was hard pressed not to reveal her amusement on occasion when some of the animals displayed distinctly uncooperative tendencies. There were also events for the children, she was surprised to realise. Some of those taking part were no more than ten years old or so, as well as a combination of both sexes, but just as eager as their older counterparts to try their luck in the ring, in their case on considerably smaller animals, though, and with the added protection of hard riding-caps on their heads and a couple of the men keeping pace alongside to ensure they came to no harm.

During the afternoon the flying doctor put in an appearance to see how everything was progressing, to watch some of the contests, check out a couple of competitors who were still feeling some effect from heavy falls, and then depart sooner than anticipated on receiving a call over the radio for urgent medical attention elsewhere.

Farrell, along with Braden and Trent, and a number of other men, spent most of the day in the arena, picking up riders once their time on their particular horse or bullock was concluded, herding the animals to and from the yards outside, and bringing their stockwhips into play when some of the cattle proved exceptionally intractable.

It was late in the afternoon before the rodeo was concluded and the relevant prizes presented—Marti's participation therein being without embarrassment on this occasion—the sun starting to slip towards the horizon and the trees stretching fragmented shadows across the cleared ground that still retained a lot of the heat that had been so intense at midday. Then came the packing up, and amid sociable farewells and happy calls of, 'We'll see you next year!' a steady stream of vehicles and planes began to make their departures.

Returning to the homestead afterwards Marti was surprised when Farrell suddenly ranged up beside her and matched his loose-limbed stride to hers. She had presumed he would have been occupied at the yards for some time yet.

'Had a good day?' he enquired idly. Except for a brief word at breakfast, it was the only time they'd spoken all day.

Remembering her overnight decision, she hunched a deprecatory shoulder. 'It was all right, I guess, if you're into all that heavily physical activity.'

His ebony-lashed eyes narrowed slightly. 'So we're back to that again, are we?' he drawled with sardonic overtones.

'I don't know what you mean,' she prevaricated. 'How can it be *back* to anything? It's the first time I've ever seen a rodeo.' She went on quickly without giving him time to reply. 'How come you're heading for the house now, anyway? Is all the work finished at the yards?'

'Not yet. I just gave myself an early mark,' he shrugged. Then he flicked her a meaningful glance. 'In order to ensure everything's ready for tomorrow.'

'Tomorrow?' she frowned. 'What's on tomorrow?'

He arched a mocking brow. 'You still have two properties to inspect, remember? Or have you changed your mind about that too?'

'No, I haven't changed my mind about it,' she denied, purposely ignoring that significant 'too'. 'I simply hadn't realised we would be leaving so soon, that's all. You could have given me more warning.'

'How was I to know any would be necessary? In your anxiety to return to the city as rapidly as humanly possible, I would have thought you'd be raring to go at the earliest opportunity.'

'Well, naturally I am, of—of course,' Marti asserted, if not quite as convincingly as she would have liked. 'So how long will this inspection take, then?'

'At a guess, four or five days,' negligently.

'Sleeping on the ground again, I suppose?' she couldn't help but grimace.

'Where else?' Farrell seemed to take pleasure in countering. 'Or were you expecting to find a five-star hotel out there?'

'Nothing so agreeable!' she was goaded into snapping. Then, recalling she still had to sound him out regarding her father's proposition, she continued in a more composed vein, 'You'll also be wanting to make an early start, I presume?' Did anyone in the bush ever do anything but?

Apparently not, she deduced, for he didn't even bother to reply. He merely slanted her a sideways speaking glance that said it all, ironically, and she sighed. They would be leaving at sunrise.

And so they did. Marti was sorry at having to say farewell to Jessica who, along with the rest of her family, would be returning home that day, but she recorded the other girl's address and promised to keep in touch this time.

'So which property will we be visiting first?' she enquired flatly of Farrell once they had left the homestead, by a different track from the one they had used when arriving, and its assortment of waving figures behind.

'Raeburn,' came the reply.

'And we'll arrive when?'

He kept his eyes on the road. 'Late this afternoon,

most probably. I've advised Vic and Dulcie we're coming.'

'Oh? Who are they?' Her winged brows arched a little higher.

Now he did flick a glance in her direction, disparagingly. 'Vic and Dulcie Ellis. The present owners, of course. Or did you think they'd simply walked off and left it vacant?' Up went his own expressive brows this time.

'How was I to know?' Marti retaliated defensively. Actually, she hadn't given the matter any thought at all, if he did but know. 'I've never inspected any properties with a view to purchase before! It could have been vacant for all I knew!' A sudden, hopeful, thought ensued. 'But since it isn't, then I guess there'll be no need . . .'

'Don't get your hopes up,' Farrell cut in on her to counsel mockingly, shrewdly anticipating exactly what was going through her mind. 'We won't be staying at the homestead, all the same.' He paused, the chafing expression etching its way across his face evident even in profile. 'Dulcie did extend an invitation for us to do so, but apart from not wanting to put her to the extra trouble, I explained how anxious you were to see as much of the place as possible, and naturally that couldn't be accomplished by remaining close to the house all the time.'

She sucked in a wrathful breath. The brute! He was back to being determined she was going to rough it, no matter what! 'And doubtless the same will also apply when we reach Leawarra,' she surmised with vexed tartness.

'You guessed it,' he drawled with a slow, lazy smile that, to her exasperation, had her pulse fluttering disconcertingly.

Damn her capricious senses, Marti fumed irritably. Didn't they realise their wayward responses were neither wanted nor appreciated? With a disgruntled sigh, she sank into silence, turning her attention elsewhere.

A couple of times they passed areas smouldering with brush fires. Once, where a burnt tree had fallen across the track, they had even been forced into pushing through the bush in order to blaze their own path around it—and thereby create a new track for those behind to follow, Marti deduced sardonically, for they had come across other similar little detours previously.

'They should be made to move those trees off the road,' she was pushed into contending when, for the second time, they had needed to find a new route past another one.

'Who should be?' countered Farrell casually.

'Those people doing the controlled burn, of course,' she returned testily, not averse to showing she wasn't altogether ignorant of all practices in the bush. They had to burn off in some of the heavily bushed outskirts of cities too.

'Except that these don't happen to be controlled burns,' he advised wryly. 'They're just spontaneous outbreaks. We get quite a number of them during the dry season.'

'Oh!' She began gazing at the smouldering, smoking undergrowth with considerably less complacency now. 'Aren't they dangerous, then?'

Farrell shrugged off-handedly. 'They can be if there's a strong wind blowing. But when it's hot and still like today, they're usually restricted to just the undergrowth and the base of the trees until they burn themselves out.'

Marti nodded, losing a little of her apprehension,

but glad when the area was finally left behind, nevertheless.

As predicted, they reached Raeburn about three-thirty in the afternoon. The homestead Marti immediately assessed as neat and unpretentious; the out-buildings few, but seemingly in a reasonable state of repair; and the Ellis family, all seven of them, whom she also thought she remembered vaguely from the rodeo, proving to be very friendly and hospitable. So much so, in fact, that Marti could only press her lips together in patent dissatisfaction when Farrell declined yet again an invitation for them to stay at the homestead while they were conducting their inspection.

'No, thanks, Dulcie,' he smiled and shook his head. 'It's very kind of you, but we don't want to inconvenience you at all.' He paused, a provoking light glinting in his eyes as they connected briefly with sparkling green. 'In any case, coming from the city as she does, Marti's finding this sleeping out something of a novelty.'

Novelty wasn't precisely the right word for it, thought Marti amid the ensuing comments and smiles of understanding from the others present, the children in particular, but before she had a chance to say so, Farrell rose lithely from the table where they'd had afternoon tea and began speaking again.

'But now I guess it's time for us to be making tracks.' He turned to the tall, lean man beside him who had also gained his feet. 'You said there's a good place to camp a few miles to the right of the river crossing, Vic?'

'Mmm, that's right,' endorsed the older man, starting to lead the way outside. 'You'll see the track leading down there just after you climb the bank.'

Farrell nodded and, making his farewells, headed

for the Cruiser. Marti, perforce, had little choice but to do the same, albeit it in a less nonchalant frame of mind.

'I don't see why we couldn't have stayed,' she put forward in grumbling tones as soon as they were on their way again. 'Dulcie did make the suggestion voluntarily, after all.'

'And maybe I just considered a few nights in the bush would be less of an inconvenience to you, than it would be adding to her workload,' Farrell returned impassively. 'Or don't you think she has enough to do already, caring for seven?'

She hunched away from the question defensively. 'I—well—I probably could have helped.'

'With what? The cooking?' he asked cynically.

Marti glared at him balefully. 'So just because I can't cook, personally, doesn't also make me incapable of following directions, you know!' she gibed.

'That's good,' he promptly smiled with such evident satisfaction that she was instantly wary. 'Because then you'll be able to lend a hand with our dinner tonight instead, won't you?'

Would she? Marti had other ideas on the matter, but tactfully decided against voicing them. Instead, she merely offered on a deliberately whimsical note, 'If that's what you want.' And she had the satisfaction of seeing his expression turn just a little doubtful for once.

By the time they had set up camp and washed, the sun was just setting and on her way back from her shower Marti stopped for a moment to gaze in silent appreciation of the stunning display as brilliant red and gold and orange streaks and swirls began to spread across the inky velvet backdrop of the sky. Somehow she found the sight soothing—perhaps because being on such a grand scale it made everything else appear inconsequential by comparison, she mused—but whatever the reason, when she resumed walking she was feeling more at ease than she had done for some time.

The first thing she noted on approaching the fire was that their meal was already well under way, and her lips twitched irrepressibly. 'I thought I was supposed to help with dinner,' she murmured, innocently tongue-in-cheek.

'Hmm.' The humorously dry look Farrell bestowed on her had her heart skipping a beat. 'I decided to trade assistance for edibility,' he drawled.

'Chicken!' she dared to taunt a laugh, flipping her fingers beneath the brim of his ever-present hat as she passed him, and tipping it down over his eyes.

Then immediately she wished she hadn't, because the lazy, totally beguiling grin that swept the corners of his mouth upwards as he righted his headgear had her heart reacting far more tempestuously than merely missing a beat. Now it first leapt to her throat, then pounded raggedly against her ribs, and she hurried on to put her toilet articles away and hang her towel on a convenient bush to dry in the hope of gaining time to recover.

That she did eventually manage to do so, Marti considered no mean feat, particularly after forcing herself to face the fact that she really didn't like the role she had chosen to play. She would have much preferred it to have been otherwise, but did she actually have a choice if she wanted to ensure the undoubted attraction Farrell held for her on occasion was never again revealed quite so plainly as it had been the night of the dance? Deciding that, since there was no discord between them at the moment, she

should make an effort to see that it continued that way
for at least one night, if only for her father's sake, she
returned to the fire determinedly.

'Do you realise that's the first river we've crossed
that's actually had water in it,' she remarked wryly
some time later while they were eating. In truth, at the
time she had been a bit nervous at the thought of
crossing it at all in view of its depth, but as Farrell had
displayed no such qualms she had done her best to
suppress her own, and in the end it hadn't presented
any difficulties whatsoever.

'Mmm,' he acknowledged laconically. 'Although
from here north you'll find they're all like that. And
the water's quite sweet to drink, if you feel so
inclined.'

He was meaning, as opposed to black tea, she
suspected drily. Aloud, she conceded, 'I thought it
might be. It's certainly as clear as crystal. I could see
the fish in it quite easily when I was showering.'
Halting, she eyed him meaningfully. 'But no crocodiles! I did remember to look for them this time.'

'Good girl,' he commended indolently, and she had
to fight down the stupidly pleased feeling that
overcome her on receiving his approval for once. 'It
never pays to take anything for granted in the bush.'

Marti looked down at the river uncertainly, dark
now except for the faint tinge of colours still painted
on it by the disappearing sunset. 'So would there be
any in there?'

'Oh, there's more than likely a few freshies—
freshwater ones,' Farrell granted matter-of-factly. 'But
you can even swim in with them and they won't give
you any trouble. It's only the salties—saltwater, or
esturarine crocodiles—that you need worry about.
However, don't let the name saltwater give you the

idea they're only found in tidal areas, because they inhabit freshwater lagoons and the like just as readily.'

She shivered and looked at him askance. 'Are you trying to make me feel better or worse?'

'Rather, preparing you for what's to come, because it's more than probable there *are* salties on Leawarra.'

'Oh, that is welcome news,' she joked hollowly. 'Are you absolutely positive we have to go there?'

Farrell flexed a muscular shoulder, his lips taking on an oblique tilt. 'I think you know the answer to that one even better than I do, sweetheart.'

Marti gave a resigned sigh and returned her attention to her meal. No, of course she didn't have any option but to go—although right at the moment she was even less keen than she had ever been!

Once dinner was concluded and their utensils cleaned, Marti accepted the cup of tea Farrell poured for her from the billy, although not without an eloquent look, and sat with it cupped between her hands as she leant back against the trunk of the massive tree behind them and let her thoughts wander.

That there really was a peaceful quality to the Peninsula, she had to admit, was her first unconscious musing. It was so clean and unspoiled, the air so clear—except when the billowing dust hung in it like a red veil, of course, she qualified drily—the water fresh and possessed of an unbelievable sparkling clarity.

Taking a sip from her mug, her reverie was broken by a large group of flying foxes, or fruit bats, winging their way noisily overhead and she looked up to watch their black outlines cross the now midnight blue, star-studded sky. Earlier, she recalled, they had even had a bandicoot come to investigate the camp quite fearlessly, and with total unconcern sit devouring the bread and apple they plied it with.

About to take another mouthful of tea, Marti only then remembered her first, and an expressive curve caught at her mouth on realising that her taste buds hadn't rebelled. Good grief, she *was* becoming accustomed to the stuff, she smiled ruefully. Then the sudden flaring of the fire as Farrell moved to squat beside it in order to add more wood drew her gaze in his direction and had her studying him surreptitiously.

In the flickering glow of the flames his darkly tanned skin gleamed like burnished copper, his profile outlined clearly, enabling her to scrutinise it slowly, and to note once again the straight nose, the strong determined jaw, the firm and shapely mouth, the hazel eyes now glinting with golden lights set within thick, sable lashes. He was every inch a man; strong, self-assured, and she didn't doubt, as dependable as destiny. If she had met him under more favourable circumstances—in the city, for instance—she probably would have . . . Choking back a gasp at the direction her meanderings were taking her, Marti applied a brake to them resolutely, furiously, and sought desperately for something else to replace them. To her relief, the thought occurred that now would be a most suitable time to mention her father's proposal.

'Have you only ever worked on Tullagindi, Farrell?' she therefore began hurriedly.

'Apart from a couple of years spent jackarooing on Avara for old Archie Butler soon after I finished school,' he supplied evenly, resuming his seat on his rolled swag and picking up his own mug again.

Marti's eyes widened slightly, her curiosity side-tracking her. 'Why would you be a jackaroo on someone else's property when your own father has one?'

He shrugged, his mouth curving crookedly. 'It's

often the custom. I guess it's figured you pay more attention to a stranger, and therefore learn more, plus providing extra experience, of course. It also ensures that, since jackaroos are normally somewhere near the bottom of the pecking order, you don't escape doing any of the unpleasant work just because you happen to be the boss's son.'

'I see,' she nodded. 'And did you? Learn more, I mean.'

'Oh, yes,' he half laughed, even white teeth shining startlingly white against the darkness of his face. 'Old Archie was nothing if not a hard taskmaster. But being one of the real old-time bushmen, he also knew his business. He could read the country and cattle better than just about anyone I've ever known—and that includes my own father, who's no slouch at the game—and he had all the skills necessary to survive in the bush. He knew it all because he'd done it all, and mostly the hard way. He was a great teacher.'

As well as a man he obviously respected, it wasn't difficult for Marti to deduce. However, as much as she unexpectedly found she would have liked to have heard more on the subject, she did have other avenues to pursue.

'Although you've never considered working on another property since that time?' she probed.

Farrell hunched a broad shoulder again. 'There's never been any reason to.'

'But if there were, would you consider it?'

He fixed her with a narrowing, speculative gaze. 'What makes you ask?' he countered instead of answering.

She took a deep, steadying breath, wanting only to do her best for her father. 'Because Daddy wanted me to ask you if you would be interested in—in managing on his behalf any property he might buy up here. If he does decide to go ahead with the idea, that is.'

Not by so much as a blink did Farrell reveal his reaction to the proposal—much to Marti's disappointment, and some little dismay. She had expected to receive at least some sign as to what he might have been thinking. Instead, he merely drawled with a hint of mockery, 'Well, well, that's taken a while to surface, hasn't it?'

Marti shifted a trifle awkwardly. 'An—umm—opportune moment never seemed to present itself previously.' How could it? Their periods of accord had been few and far between.

A muscle flickered briefly at the side of his jaw, then stilled. 'So that's what occasioned this evening's abrupt change in manner of yours, is it?' A hardening note entered his voice.

'No!' The denial burst from her swiftly. Honesty, if not diplomacy, made her amend discomfitedly, 'Well, not entirely.' She hurried on. 'I just thought that during our inspection of the properties would probably be the—the most appropriate time, that's all.'

Whether he believed her or not was impossible to tell because his expression was inscrutable, and she touched her teeth to her lip apprehensively. She hadn't inadvertently ruined her parent's chances, after all, had she?

'Or, put another way better late than never, hmm?' Farrell surmised cynically at length.

The conjecture was too shrewdly accurate for Marti's comfort, but simultaneously she didn't think all the blame was hers either. 'So what was I supposed to do? Try and fit it in between all your criticisms of me?' she flared tartly. 'I hardly think you would have been in the mood to give the idea your unbiased consideration if I had!'

'And you actually cared whether I did or not?'

'Yes, I did! Because even though you may choose to believe otherwise, I'll have you know I do happen to think the world of my father, and I really did want to do my very best on his behalf?' Halting, she dropped her gaze to the mug in her hands, her voice lowering to a despondent murmur. 'Only now it appears I've failed him in that too.'

'I don't know why you'd think that,' Farrell suprised her by declaring in roughened tones. 'Unless you're trying to pre-empt my decision, of course.'

'You mean, you *are* interested in the proposition?' Marti held her breath hopefully.

He inclined his head in a speculative gesture. 'I could be, depending on the terms and conditions.'

Her initial feeling of relief was replaced by one of indecisiveness. 'I don't know those. Daddy only asked me to sound you out as to whether you would consider taking it on.' She glanced across at him with a shyness she hadn't experienced for years. 'He—he apparently values your judgment very highly.'

'Which is more than can be said of his daughter,' he said drily.

With her spirits restored, Marti was able to retort in kind. 'And perhaps if you restricted your judgments to cattle and the like, maybe I would too.'

This forecast she certainly discovered to have been more prophetic than she realised, or intended, during the next few days as they conducted their inspection of first Raeburn and then Leawarra, because the more time she spent with him, the more Marti did come to appreciate his opinions—and his company, the latter decidedly to her consternation at times.

She also found herself drawn more to the second property as well, although in her case she suspected it was more its aesthetic appeal than its potential that attracted her on reaching the old homestead. In a state of disrepair it might have been, but it was also part of one of the prettiest scenes she thought she had ever seen. Set high above another of the area's crystal-clear rivers as it tumbled downwards some fifty feet or more by way of a succession of pandanus and palm-surrounded rock pools, it looked more like the setting for a tourist resort than a cattle station, Marti decided wryly.

'Well, I told you it was run down, didn't I?' remarked Farrell expressively as they walked back to the Land Cruiser after having been invited inside for a cup of tea by the property's frail and white-haired owners.

'But it has such character!' Marti claimed enthusiastically, glancing back at the long lattice-shaded verandahs overhung with brightly flowering vines, the wide plank walls, the decorated ventilators capping the low hip roof. 'Did you realise all those walls are made of cedar?'

He nodded. 'That's why it's still free of termites, and it's mostly only in need of repair rather than replacement.' He cast her a quizzical look. 'But how did you know it was cedar? Most of it has been painted over.'

'I know—and what a crime!' She gazed skywards eloquently. 'But it had peeled and flaked in enough places for me to see what was behind it and, as it so happens, because interior decorating and renovation is a pet hobby of mine, I've learnt to recognise quite a few timbers over the years. So, you see, my life in the city hasn't been entirely unproductive,' she gibed with a smile on reaching the vehicle and swinging on to the seat.

'Then why don't you do something constructive with the knowledge, instead of just playing with it?' he suggested implicitly as he slid in beside her.

'Make a career of it, you mean?' She shook her head. 'I'd probably have to work to set hours, then, and perhaps even be involved in a number of projects at the same time, and I don't think I'd like that. I prefer to be able to devote all my time and attention to the one undertaking until it's completed. Besides,' she slanted him a humorous, taunting glance, 'what makes you think I'm good enough to make a success of it commercially?'

'Because from what I've seen so far, I'd say there was enough of your father's determination in you to make a success of anything, *if* all that wasted persistence could just be channelled into something worthwhile, that is!' he contended in ironic accents as he set the Cruiser into motion.

At best, it was a backhanded compliment, mused Marti ruefully, and yet the fact that he had still found *something* about her commendable had her experiencing a surge of pleasurable warmth out of all proportion to what should have been its importance.

'Yes—well . . .' She hunched a diffident shoulder, trying to rid herself of the self-conscious feeling, and reverted to their original topic in the hope of doing so. 'I still think that homestead has tremendous promise. In fact, should Daddy buy Leawarra, I might even give him some ideas concerning its improvement. With the paint stripped, the timber sanded and polished, a few additions and alterations here and there, a couple of Persian carpets on the floors . . .'

'In a manager's house?' Farrell interposed, arching a sceptical brow.

Marti caught at her lip with pearly white teeth, her cheeks starting to burn at the realisation she had been picturing it with herself in occupation. 'Well—er—maybe not exactly Persian carpets. Even Daddy's known consideration as an employer might not extend that far,' she pushed out along with a shaky laugh in an effort to hide her embarrassment. 'It was just a—a general impression I was trying to create, n-not an actual one.' A brief pause, and she deviated slightly in the hope of diverting him, 'I suppose it's due to their age that the Touhills are selling?'

'Uh-huh!' he confirmed laconically, although only after having subjected her to a measuring scrutiny that had her speculating discomfitedly that he was well aware of her intention. 'They never had any sons, only three daughters, and they've all long since married and moved elsewhere.'

'None of their husbands—or children, if it comes to that—are interested in working the property?'

'Presumably not,' he shrugged. 'It happens that way sometimes.'

'I suppose so,' Marti allowed absently, her thoughts already moving on. 'And Vic and Dulcie Ellis? I must admit their wanting to sell intrigued me a little when they seemed perfectly content with Raeburn really.'

'Yes, well, in their case it's somewhat different, because although it's not all that noticeable as yet, I understand one of their kids has been shown to have a medical problem that requires regular examinations and specialised treatment. And ill health is something isolated regions don't allow for, I'm afraid. So they're selling in order to move to a centre where they can obtain the necessary treatment without all the upheaval and extra expense that's involved every few weeks at present.'

'How tragic for them,' she sympathised, subsiding into a saddened silence for a time. The talk of leaving properties had engendered another thought, however, and after a while she raised it. 'If you did agree to manage a property for Daddy, Farrell, wouldn't you have any reservations about leaving Tullagindi? I mean, since you're the eldest I assume it will be yours one day, and that being so, I would have thought you'd have preferred working on what is as good as your own property rather than just managing one for someone else.'

He flicked her a chaffing glance. 'Is that your way of trying to get me to reconsider?'

'No!' she protested, aghast. Then she shook her head in mild exasperation on seeing the amusement in his eyes. 'And I'm being serious!'

'Sorry,' he grinned, his mouth curving into a heart-stopping smile, and not evincing the least sign of penitence. 'For your information, though, Tullagindi will never be solely mine or Braden's—unless one of us buys the other out—because it will be a joint ownership. As for the other, well, I did say it all depended on the terms and conditions, and I'm really only interested in getting whichever property Harry purchases producing to the best of its capabilities and then handing over to someone else.'

'Y-you s-still h-haven't s-said w-why,' she persisted, the uncontrollable shake in her voice brought about by the shuddering of the vehicle as they lurched and thumped across some deep ruts.

Farrell shrugged, his lips twisting wryly. 'I guess you could say, the challenge. It's a whole lot more

satisfying improving something and making it grow
than merely keeping it running smoothly.'

'You sound just like my father!'

'Perhaps it's a Peninsula characteristic.'

To take fate by the horns and mould it to their will?
He certainly would, that she didn't doubt! The
slowing of the engine suddenly distracted her and she
gazed outside curiously. 'Why are we stopping?'

'So you can take some more photos for Harry to
peruse. Remember?' he said drily.

Marti smiled widely and waited until he had
retrieved her camera from the back, as usual. 'What of
this time?' she asked blithely. The same as she had
been doing ever since their first afternoon on Raeburn
when it had become abundantly obvious she really
didn't have any idea as to what her father would
consider important and of interest, from which time
she had left all such decisions for Farrell to make, as
now. Stepping down to the ground, she waved a hand
in the direction of some charred and dilapidated
fencing. 'More of the state of the fences?'

Farrell's expression assumed a long-suffering cast,
and by the simple expedient of grasping the nape of
her neck, turned her ninety degrees to her left. 'How
about those cattle over there? He'd be interested in the
condition of his prospective stock, don't you reckon?'

'Mmm, I suppose so,' she owned on a rueful note
and dutifully recorded the animals in question. 'Is that
all?' She glanced up with an impish look on her face.

The grip on her neck tightened imperceptibly. 'Try
the cleared area beyond the trees,' he growled.

Repressing a laugh, she did as directed and then
turned sparkling emerald eyes upwards again. 'Anything else?' she enquired mirthfully.

For a time his gaze remained fixed to her vivacious

features, and then he released her and moved away abruptly. 'Not of relevance,' he replied in shortening tones as he prepared to take his place behind the wheel once more.

With her demeanour changing rapidly to one of bafflement, Marti replaced her camera in the back and resumed her own seat, her thoughts in turmoil. What had she done now, she wondered confusedly. Inadvertently reminded him with her bantering remarks of just how out of place she was in the bush? But he had always known that, and no matter what the reason, why should his sudden reversal in attitude have caused her such an acute stab of pain, anyway?

The slight digression in her train of thought had Marti sucking in a sharp breath, her hands clenching, but despite all her efforts to disregard it, it remained firmly implanted in the forefront of her mind, overshadowing every other consideration. Oh, what was the use in trying to pretend otherwise—she was in love with him, she was forced into admitting finally. Contrary to what her head had attempted to tell her that first night on Raeburn, it seemed it hadn't mattered where she had met him, after all, because somehow he had managed to capture her heart just the same.

Not that there was any of the joy she had always expected to be related to such a discovery, however. For just as it was obvious to her now why he'd had such an effect on her senses at times, it was also equally evident there was very little likelihood of anything ever coming of it, she realised in despair. Not only was she still unsure she even wanted to alter her lifestyle so radically as actually to live in the bush, she was even less certain that she *could* do so successfully!

All of which was quite apart from the fact that there

was no guarantee Farrell was ever likely to reciprocate her feelings, or more importantly, even if he did, would be willing to take such a gamble on someone who didn't only show a distinct ineptitude for his way of life, but had deliberately set out to display a dislike of it as well—even on those occasions when the opposite had been the case. This was something she deeply regretted now, but simultaneously surmised it was a little too late to begin claiming differently. No, she decided miserably, if Farrell ever took a woman into his life it would be someone like Jess, definitely not someone like herself!

For the remainder of the day they continued with their tour of Leawarra mainly in silence. Farrell displayed little inclination to talk except when necessary, and Marti was not exactly ungrateful for his unusually withdrawn behaviour. It made it less of a strain for her to act naturally, and at least appear unconcerned, in spite of the unwanted opportunities it presented her turbulent thoughts to overwhelm her.

To combat them, she began studying the country they passed through more thoroughly. She noted for the first time really how it would change from open grasslands to thick woodland; from rugged hills to broad valleys containing tranquil paperbark-lined lagoons covered with delicate waterlilies, and playing host to innumerable waterbirds of every description; from termite-mound-covered flats to dark, dense, and wet rain-forest which resounded with a variety of bird calls, the whipbird's distinctive notes sounding out clearly above the rest.

Regardless of having earlier been advised that the property extended all the way to the coast, Marti still wasn't quite prepared for the sight that greeted her late in the afternoon as they came out to a low, grassed

promontory overlooking the sea. In either direction
the dazzlingly white sand, untouched and deserted,
stretched as far as the eye could see, lapped by clear
azure water on one side and edged with tall, swaying
palms and tropical greenery on the other.

'Well, what do you think?' Farrell turned to face
her, dark brows lifting.

'It's beautiful,' she granted quietly.

'I meant, as our camping site for tonight.'

'Oh!' Her cheeks coloured lightly at the sardonic
timbre in his voice. 'Up here, or—or down on the
beach?'

'Apparently there's a small clearing between the
two, behind which there's a small creek that forms a
series of shallow rapids on its way down to the beach,'
he advised, already starting to head the vehicle
towards a deep sand track that led downwards.

'Then it sounds quite suitable, I guess,' Marti
murmured. 'Although there doesn't appear to be any
sign of an outfall from a creek anywhere.'

'No, well, that's no doubt because it seemingly
continues parallel to the beach for a way, where it
diverges into a succession of large pools which then
seep into the ground, only to bubble to the surface
again through the sand at various points along the
beach.'

'I see,' she nodded, making a mental note to look
for the bubbling outlets. She had heard of such
occurrences before, but never actually seen one.

The clearing proved to be a pretty place, although
Marti really wasn't in the mood to appreciate its
picturesque qualities to the full, nor did she speak
much as they went about their normal evening routine
of setting up camp, washing, and having dinner. She
was still none the wiser as to why Farrell had changed

so suddenly, although in a way she supposed she should have been thankful that he had. It was difficult enough disguising the pain and confusion she was experiencing now, without it being made even harder by him continuing to be the engaging company he had been.

'I think I'll go for a walk,' she proposed tautly soon after their meal and washing-up was concluded, and rising to her feet, she brushed off her skirt and made for the sandy track swiftly. The tension in the air was almost palpable and she felt she just had to get away for a while.

'You'd better keep to the beach,' Farrell counselled brusquely behind her.

Marti lifted a hand in acknowledgement and continued downwards on bare feet to the hard-packed, smooth sand below. He considered it likely *she* would go wandering through the bush alone at night? she speculated ironically.

Heading for the water's edge, she walked along in the rippling shallows for a time, watching the moon rise to shed its silvery light upon the softly surging sea. Then she started up the gently sloping expanse of the beach again, those areas of wet sand leading her directly to where tiny scoops had been formed by the water from the creek as it bubbled slowly to the surface.

On discovering more of the outlets, she followed them to the low, brush and creeper-covered foreshore, wondering how far distant were the pools that Farrell had mentioned. She stepped over the creepers gingerly, peering into the darkness beyond, and heard a rustling sound followed by a noise that was somewhere between a loud hiss and a snarl that had her blood freezing in her veins as it reverberated in the quiet night air. Crocodile!

'*Marti!*' Farrell's resonant voice, carrying a note of urgency, reached her almost immediately afterwards, indicating he had heard it too, and spurred her into action.

Whirling about, she cleared the creepers in one leap and, hitching up her skirt, went flying along the beach as fast as her legs could carry her. Just knowing those reptiles were quite able of running faster than a human being had her heart pounding even harder than her feet—God, how far had she walked?—but she didn't dare turn to look in case that slowed her, and it just wasn't possible to hear anything over her own increasingly laboured breathing.

Farrell, moving even faster from the other direction, met her just as Marti thought her legs were about to collapse, and she flew straight into his arms for safety like a homing pigeon to its cote.

'I told you to keep to the beach!' he promptly blazed at her angrily.

It was doubtful Marti could have answered even if she had wanted to—her breath was still coming in shuddering gasps—and so she merely continued to sag against him weakly, her arms clinging about his back, her legs threatening to stop supporting her.

Farrell muttered an explosive expletive, bent slightly to swing her effortlessly into his arms, and began striding back towards their camp site. Only too relieved not to have to make it under her own steam, Marti wound her arms tightly around his neck and buried her head against a muscular shoulder, shivering at the narrowness of her escape.

By the time they reached the camp, her breathing had almost returned to normal, but when he set her feet to the ground, reaction had her continuing to hold on to him convulsively. He represented strength and security, and right at the moment she felt the need for both.

When one restrained attempt to extricate himself from her grasp proved in vain, Farrell expelled a long breath, appearing to relent, and some of the tenseness left him as his arms encircled her comfortingly. 'You should have kept to the beach,' he sighed softly.

Marti burrowed closer, an involuntary shudder escaping her. 'I know, I know. I'm sorry,' she whispered shakily. 'I just didn't think.' Stiffening suddenly, she pulled back a little, looking about the clearing fearfully. 'One couldn't reach us here, could it? After all, the creek is at the back there, and— and . . .'

'Sssh!' He laid a gentle finger across her lips to still her words. 'There's no danger here. Apart from the fact that crocs don't wander this far from water, they always prefer still, deep water to the shallow, swiftly running kind, in any case.' He lifted a hand to cradle her head, stroking her hair reassuringly. 'So you see, you're quite safe now. There's nothing more to be afraid of.'

Her emerald eyes searched his uncertainly. 'You're not just saying that?'

His mouth sloped crookedly and he dropped a light kiss on her forehead. 'No, I'm not just saying that.' A pause. 'Or don't you trust me?'

She nodded, a shy half-smile shaping her tender mouth. She would trust him with her life if necessary. 'I also thank you for your help.' She reached up impulsively to lay her lips against the corner of his shapely mouth.

Immediately the atmosphere seemed charged with electricity as their gazes connected and held, then as if something were compelling him, Farrell dragged her to him roughly. 'Damn you, Marti!' he rasped in a deep voice as his mouth claimed hers with an urgent hunger.

Recovering from her initial surprise, Marti's reaction was soon as compulsive as his as she gave of herself freely, her body melting against his, her lips responding fervently to his exhilarating demands. She felt a pervasive heat course through her, inflaming her senses, scorching her with its depth, and she gave a long, shuddering sigh as he continued to stimulate her emotions to a degree she hadn't believed possible.

Abruptly, she realised they were on the grass, although she couldn't remember them moving there, or recall when Farrell's shirt had been discarded. Perhaps she had helped remove it, she mused dazedly, in her desire to explore the hard, ridged muscles of his chest and shoulders thus exposed, just as her sensitive fingertips were now doing, and in just the same fashion as his hands were beginning to roam over her soft, curving flesh after he adeptly disposed of her loose-fitting top.

In the pale light her rounded breasts gleamed as if gilded, the nipple hard and prominent, and she moaned helplessly as his hands leisurely, stirringly caressed every swelling inch of them, a soft sound that quickly turned to a rapturous sob when he took each thrusting nipple into his warm mouth in turn, sucking and tormenting them to even great arousal, and flooding Marti with sensations that completely overwhelmed her.

In a fever of desire she arched against him ardently, her slender arms twining tightly about his neck, her mouth meeting his again in a fiery, sensuous kiss that went beyond anything she had previously experienced. She loved him, wanted him, and no matter what happened nothing could change that.

Then suddenly, with a sharp shake of his head, Farrell swung away from her. 'It would appear I was wrong—there is danger here for you, after all . . . me!' he grated. 'I'm afraid you're a damnable temptation in any man's language, but as I hardly think my making love to his only daughter is likely to endear me to my prospective employer . . .' He took a deep breath, his expression taut. 'I'm sorry, it wasn't my intention for anything like this to happen.'

'Nor mine either,' claimed Marti throatily, only her pride sustaining her as she tried desperately to regain control of her turbulent emotions as embarrassment and anguish flooded through her. Averting her gaze, she retrieved her top and donned it hurriedly. 'It—it must have been reaction, I guess. I j-just wasn't thinking straight.' Her voice quavered uncontrollably.

'No, well, if you'd just kept to the beach as you were told,' he returned on a tight note.

'So you said earlier!' she fired back in defence of her torn and aching feelings. Oh, God, if she had needed proof that she was never likely to mean anything to him, she surely had it now! As if deliberately, remorselessly, to put the matter beyond doubt, she lifted her chin higher and made herself face him with faked unconcern. 'And doubtless you'll be more than slightly relieved to have me out of your hair once and for all when I finally return to Brisbane!'

'You're damn right I will!' he had no compunction in grinding out savagely.

Shattered by the sheer ferocity with which his confirmation had been delivered, Marti's throat worked helplessly for a second or two, and she had to press her lips together tightly to camouflage their betraying trembling. 'No more than I will, I can assure you!' she forced out at last in a strangled voice, and scrambling to her feet, she made her way across the clearing swiftly to begin unrolling her swag.

'You think I don't know that?' Farrell flung after her pungently. But with just enough of an inflection in his tone to have her steps slowing momentarily. Surely that hadn't been—bitterness?—her ears had thought they'd detected, she pondered briefly. With a shake of her head she dismissed the idea as being ridiculous. What had he got to be bitter about? She was the one to have been found wanting!

CHAPTER EIGHT

BACK in Brisbane, the next couple of months passed slowly, and not particularly enjoyably for Marti. Too often she found Farrell invading her thoughts, in spite of her determined efforts to put him firmly out of her mind and continue with her life much as before.

Not that even her lifestyle seemed to provide her with the same satisfaction as it once had, she discovered despondently, as the constant round of parties and strictly social functions with the same people present all the time began to pall a little. Did any of them actually serve a purpose, except as opportunities to destroy a few reputations—all under cover of the supposedly friendliest of smiles, of course—or to undercut opposition business deals? She found herself wondering on occasion.

The only matter to have really given her pleasure since returning was her father's obvious delight at her changed attitude towards the bush in general, and the Peninsula in particular. With him she had been quite open in admitting that her visit had neither been uninteresting, nor the total bore she had anticipated.

As a result he kept her informed concerning the progress of his proposed purchase of Raeburn and/or Leawarra, a circumstance that undoubtedly helped frustrate Marti's attempts to keep Farrell out of her thoughts, but which her heart at least was more than willing—masochistically, she speculated dolefully?—to disregard. If only she had been equally willing to confess her interest in the bush had also been stirred, she often lamented. Would it have altered anything?

She had no way of knowing, of course, but when her father unknowingly presented her with the chance to find out, she jumped at it with an unexpected alacrity that, if nothing else, proved beyond a shadow of a doubt that Farrell Stephens meant more to her than even she realised, because she suddenly knew that he had become her reason for living.

It happened one evening when her father arrived home very late after a protracted conference and found her curled up with a book, which she had been unsuccessfully attempting to read, in a large velvet-upholstered armchair in the sitting-room.

'Hello, princess, I didn't expect to see you here. I thought you'd been invited to some dinner party or the other at Zara's this evening,' Harry Grayson said as he stopped by her chair to drop a kiss on the top of her head before helping himself to a drink from the leather-fronted bar situated in one corner of the spacious room. 'Where's your mother? Gone to bed, I suppose.'

'About an hour ago,' Marti smiled. 'I decided to give Zara's party a miss in favour of a good read.'

He nodded, draping his jacket over a bar-stool and then loosening his tie and unfastening the top button of his shirt as he walked back towards her. 'Which proved to be a disappointing one, after all, hmm?' he surmised, flicking a finger at the few pages turned over as he continued on to the chair opposite.

'Something like that,' she allowed with a diffident hunching of one shoulder, and quickly changed the subject. 'So how was your day? You don't think you're overdoing it by keeping such long hours, Daddy?' Her forehead creased with concern.

'Meaning, you think I'm past it?' he quipped, and then chuckled and raised an arresting hand when she would have protested. 'No, I know you didn't mean it like that, princess. I was only teasing. Although, in a manner of speaking, I have decided to take a few days off starting Wednesday.' He took a mouthful of his drink. 'I thought I might fly up to the Peninsula for a brief look round myself before the final signing.'

'Why? There's nothing wrong with the arrangements, is there? I thought it was all settled that you were going to purchase Raeburn, and . . .' she couldn't help the imperceptible hesitation, 'Farrell was going to manage it for you.'

'No, no, all the arrangements still stand. Well, in the major sense they do,' he qualified wryly, enigmatically too, from his daughter's standpoint. 'No, I guess you could say it's really just an excuse for me to visit for a while because I missed doing so at the time of the rodeo.'

Marti nodded, relieved, and took a deep breath. 'Er—I don't suppose you'd like some company on the trip, would you?' she put forward half tentatively, half cajolingly.

'You mean, you?' And when she nodded, 'Well, of course I would!' A beaming smile lit up his craggy face. 'I can't think of anyone whose company I'd welcome more! Except your mother's, naturally,' he added diplomatically, and had them both smiling. 'I've been hoping for so long that we might make the trip together one day. You really liked it that much up there, eh?'

Marti swallowed nervously. 'Well, I'd certainly like to see it with you,' she side-stepped.

'And so you shall!' He paused, his face still split by such a wide, happy smile that Marti could only deeply regret all those other occasions when he had invited her to accompany him and she had refused so indifferently. 'Including Leawarra. You liked that property, didn't you?'

His remark also reminded her of her last night there, and her heart gave an involuntary lurch. 'It's very pretty,' she granted in a small, tight voice. 'But do you think we should call there? After all, now that you're not considering buying the place . . .' She gave a faint, but significant shrug.

Harry Grayson laughed. 'You're forgetting the new owner, aren't you?'

New owner! She stared at him in surprise, her spirits sinking. Somehow she found the idea depressing. 'What new owner?' she asked, perplexed.

'Well.' No sooner had he begun than he halted, his own expression undergoing a marked change. 'Good lord, I must have told you, surely! I know I had a lot on my mind at the time, but . . .'

'What new owner, Daddy?' Marti broke in on an anxious note.

'Well, Farrell,' he supplied at last, and much to her astonishment. 'He told me he was interested in the property himself shortly after you arrived home, so when I didn't take up the option on it, he bought it himself.' He looked at her apologetically. 'I didn't tell you?'

She shook her head, her previous depression lifting miraculously even though the furrows creasing her forehead remained. 'I wouldn't have thought he could afford it.' The words came out more bluntly than she intended.

'Neither could he altogether.' His lips twitched expressively. 'However, there are always people ready to lend money to those who show some enterprise and ability. And Farrell has both in abundance, as I've always said. He's a good risk.'

'*You* lent him the money?' Marti surmised in sudden comprehension.

'Uh-huh! Willingly,' he smiled. 'Besides, could I do less for him than his grandfather did for me when he loaned me the money for my start?'

Her green eyes widened in surprise. 'I didn't know that!'

'I've never kept it a secret,' he advised gently.

In other words, if she had been bothered to show some attention, she would have known, she deduced. It was another distressing reminder, and she went on swiftly. 'Then if he has his own property, he won't be managing Raeburn for you, after all.'

'That's what I thought, but,' he nodded approvingly, 'he's a man of his word, that one. He said he would manage it for me, and he intends to do so, at least until he's built it up and he can either find, or has trained, someone to take over from him, which was part of the deal, in any case.'

'Mmm, he said something of the kind to me,' Marti mused. 'What will happen to Leawarra in the meantime, though?'

'Well, it will involve a lot of hard work, obviously—which he certainly isn't afraid of—but he apparently believes it's possible to run the two successfully.'

She could also recall Farrell saying something similar on another occasion, and supposed he just saw it as another challenge. 'And you?' She gazed at her father enquiringly. 'Are you also satisfied it can be accomplished effectually?'

Harry Grayson pulled at an earlobe thoughtfully. 'Let's put it this way. If it can't, then I'm damn certain he'll admit as much and ensure I'm not the loser as a result. I trust him completely. He's that kind of man.'

Yes, he was, Marti acceded pensively. He was his own man—steadfast, self-reliant, resourceful—and possessed of a strength of will that would see him through any adversity. That they were also all attributes that could defeat her before she even came close to achieving her desire, she became increasingly aware, and apprehensive about, as the days passed, the more so when, on the following Wednesday afternoon, a remark of her father's warned that the end of their journey north was finally approaching.

'It won't be long now. There's Coen,' he pointed out with a smile as Vern Stephens, who had collected them at the Cairns airport, banked the small Cessna above the surrounding hills.

Marti nodded jerkily and, in the hope of diverting her own disturbing thoughts, commented, 'The country seems to look even more rugged from up here than it does from the road.'

'One of the reasons why the region's still so undeveloped,' Vern turned from the pilot's seat to impart. 'I mean, it was only thirty years ago that Coen's mail was still being delivered by pack-horse from Laura because there was no road.' A graphic smile crossed his lips. 'I might add, there still isn't once you travel further north from here. It's just a track—wash-aways, sand patches, corrugations, gullies, river crossings, and all—that's been worn into the bush by the succession of vehicles travelling it.'

'I know. I also travelled on part of it during my inspection tour,' she relayed with a drily explicit look, and once more fell to mulling over what was quickly assuming the proportions of a monumental task she had set herself.

So just what was she going to say to Farrell, she pondered in something of a panic. She could hardly just walk up to him and declare that she hadn't been strictly truthful in claiming she still had no interest in the bush whatsoever, so if he felt inclined to marry her, she was more than willing. For all she knew, it might never have crossed his mind to offer anything of the sort, anyway, irrespective of whether she liked it or not. When all was said and done, a few kisses weren't exactly a declaration of undying love.

The one memory that did help to sustain her a little—something that had returned again and again to be mused over and dissected—was that momentary touch of bitterness she had detected in his voice that devastating evening on Leawarra. It just *had* to have been prompted by something stronger than mere dissatisfaction with her supposed preference for the city, hadn't it? Or was that simply wishful thinking on her part?

Slumping, rather than leaning, back in her seat, she began chewing at her lower lip in an agony of trepidation on seeing Tullagindi come into view, her aching yearning to see Farrell again warring with a contradictory dread at the prospect.

As it happened, however, Marti soon discovered on their reaching the homestead that he wasn't even on Tullagindi, but was at Leawarra. This was information that granted her agitated emotions only a moment's brief respite before they, conversely, began clamouring against the enforced delay, a deferment that kept her in suspense for another two days during which she alternately wondered why she had come, wished she hadn't, and yet subconsciously knew she couldn't have done otherwise if there were to be any meaning at all to her life in the future.

In fact, it was only by clinging tenaciously to that last rationale that she was able to make the subsequent journey to Leawarra with any degree of certainty that she was doing the right thing. Not that it lessened her nervousness, nonetheless, when they finally arrived at the property and, on Vern Stephens taxiing the plane close to the homestead, she saw Farrell coming to meet them.

Ensuring she was the last to leave the Cessna, Marti stepped down to the ground as the men were exchanging greetings, her gaze immediately flying to the younger man whose tall, impressive figure was partly turned away from her. He was smiling at her father at the time, and her heart promptly contracted in response, all her feminine instincts stimulated by his flagrant masculinity.

'And surprise, surprise! Look who's also come with us!' she was suddenly conscious of his father saying, and she unknowingly held her breath as Farrell turned in her direction.

Briefly, his expression tightened imperceptibly, a muscle rippling at the side of his jaw, and then a sweeping glance appraised her boldly from head to toe, bringing a warm flush to her smooth cheeks. 'Well, well!' he drawled. 'So what brings you back to these parts? Suddenly developed an uncontrollable attraction to the bush, have you?'

'Well, that certainly seems to be the case where the Peninsula's concerned, at least,' put in her father happily, apparently not picking up the sardonic inference.

Thinking it just might be the very opening she had been racking her brains to find, Marti drew a deep breath and rushed into speech. 'Or, maybe, just someone who happens to live here,' she amended, forcing herself to hold Farrell's glance unwaveringly. If he concluded she was meaning himself, then the remark would have to draw *some* reaction to indicate just what his feelings might be, wouldn't it, his less than encouraging greeting notwithstanding. While if he supposed she was implying someone else, well, that could hopefully prove enlightening too.

The response she received, though, wasn't quite what she had hoped for.

'Well, how about that!' exclaimed Vern Stephens in surprise.

'You never mentioned anything like that to me!' was her father's equally incredulous contribution.

'Such as?' Farrell probed baldly, his expression watchful rather than revealing.

Marti gave her golden hair a toss and carefully composed her features into a provoking smile. 'That, I'm afraid, will have to remain my secret for the present because I'm not even certain anything will come of it yet,' she replied with an airiness she was far from feeling, and hastily began making for the house in the hope of thwarting any further questions on the subject.

'Well, that's something, at least,' she heard her father sigh thankfully behind her. 'Have you any idea as to who this bloke might be, Vern?'

What was said in return she never heard, because a more perturbing voice sounded much closer at hand. 'Just what the hell are you playing at, Marti?' demanded Farrell tersely. 'You know bloody well not a damn thing interested you while you were here!'

'Didn't it?' she countered valiantly. 'Or perhaps I just pretended it didn't.'

'Oh, don't give me that!' His voice lowered to a savage mutter due to the two men following. 'You made your feelings unmistakably clear ... about everything!'

'Then if that was the case, why would I have asked—*asked*,' she repeated in emphasising accents, 'if I could accompany Daddy when he came?'

'God only knows! But it sure wasn't because you liked the region, or anyone who lives here!' He uttered a low, scoffing half-laugh. 'You didn't even spend enough time with any man here to become interested in one of them!'

Except him, of course, but he seemed to have forgotten that. She licked at her lips uneasily, fearing she was being pushed further than she had intended going, but feeling she had to give her story a little more credit. 'N-not even Trent?' she put forward jerkily. 'After all, he was there at ...'

'Trent!' He cut in on her incredulously, furiously. Without warning, he suddenly turned to call over his shoulder to the pair walking more slowly behind them. 'I just want to ask Marti's advice about something regarding the house. You go ahead and have a look over the outbuildings. We won't be long.' And catching hold of her arm in an inescapable, inflexible grip, he propelled her up the steps and into the homestead before she even had a chance to object or resist.

Once inside he released her almost immediately, his hands dropping to rest on lean hips as he eyed her intently from between narrowing lids. 'Okay, so just what are you up to, sweetheart?' he grated.

Marti's own gaze flickered warily. 'I don't know what you mean.'

He bent a little closer. 'I mean, I happen to *know* just how few were the exchanges you had with Trent! Not to mention the fact that he also just happened to spend the majority of his time in some entirely different female's company!'

She hadn't realised. 'I—well . . .' She took a step backwards, feeling a trifle unnerved by his proximity, and sought protection in attempted hauteur. 'I'm not answerable to you, in any case, and—and nor is it any concern of yours either!'

'No?' Up went two sardonically peaking brows. 'Then perhaps you shouldn't have chosen to abruptly reappear out of the blue on *my* property in order to expound your highly unlikely theories!' Pausing, his lips curled derisively. 'Or was the spoilt little socialite just so damned bored that she was willing to say and do *anything* in order to provide herself with an amusing diversion?'

'That's not true!' she denied, her eyes shading with despair that he should evidently believe her capable of behaving in such a manner. 'And—and at least my father doesn't think the same as you, thankfully. Or didn't you hear what he said?'

'I heard.' He was significantly unimpressed. 'But then, you've never experienced any difficulty in wrapping him around your little finger one way or another, have you? And neither does it explain your reference to Trent!'

Caught in a trap of her own making, Marti shifted from one foot to the other uncomfortably. 'Which appears to hold an inordinate amount of interest for you, apparently!' she burst out in defence. 'Anyone would think you were his keeper!'

'In view of your statements, he could perhaps very well need one!' Farrell retorted grimly.

'So you're being very altruistic and electing yourself to the role, hmm?'

'He happens to be a friend, and I wouldn't want to

see him caught in your destructive toils!'

Strangely, despite its cutting content, the remark had Marti's spirits beginning to lift for the first time. Somehow it just hadn't sounded right. In her experience, men simply didn't interfere to such a degree on another's behalf when it came to affairs with the opposite sex. They were far more likely to utter a rueful, 'Poor devil, he doesn't know what he's letting himself in for,' or something similar, and leave him to make the best of it; particularly, she would have thought, where someone like Trent Dunbar was concerned, who certainly hadn't ever struck her as being either sufficiently inexperienced or incapable of dealing quite satisfactorily with any such matters himself.

It was a reasoning that, if correct, left the way open to a distinctly more desirable possibility, and with her fingers figuratively crossed, if not literally, she impetuously decided to play her hunch.

'So who's going to protect the keeper?' She slanted a provocative glance at him from beneath long, curling lashes.

A hard-eyed, ominous mask fell over his features. 'And just what's that supposed to mean?'

She inclined her head winsomely and trailed a forefinger down the front of his drill shirt lightly. 'I didn't think you were that imperceptive,' she teased with a piquant smile.

'Go to hell, Marti!' Farrell exploded harshly, gripping her wrist in a painful clasp that had her wincing involuntarily and her assurance slipping a notch. 'Or better still, go back to Brisbane and relieve your boredom with some other poor sucker down there! I don't need you in my life blowing hot and cold as the mood takes you!' He flung her arm away from his dismissively.

It took all the willpower Marti possessed to retain any of her composure at all, let alone pretend to be unaffected by his rebuff. She had never had to suffer such a thing in her life before. 'You did the same in mine,' she felt entitled to remind him, the huskiness in her voice something she couldn't control.

'Then you're doubtless grateful knowing I won't be doing so again in the future!' He turned as if to leave.

'Because you're not interested?' She only just managed to push out the hardest words she had ever had to say.

Farrell pulled up short, dragging his hat from his head and slapping it violently against a solid thigh before swinging back to face her again. 'Just what are you trying to say, Marti?' he ground out in taut tones.

She swallowed hard and painfully, her courage on the point of deserting her. 'Oh, what does it sound like, you blind, obstinate, impossible great idiot!' she half flared, half choked, his image becoming blurred with unshed tears. 'Why else do you think I came back here, and put myself through this? Of course it wasn't because of Trent!' She drew a shuddering breath. 'It was because of *you*! Because I love you, you damned infuriating—you damned . . .!' Her voice cracked and she about-turned, covering her face with her hands, unable to continue.

Tossing his hat on to a nearby chair, Farrell took three swift strides, and then she was encased within strong arms. 'I think I've got the message,' he murmured deeply against the top of her head. 'I'm sorry, I just couldn't fathom why you were here, and had even less of an idea as to how I was going to endure watching you leave again! All I could think was, hell, how I love and need that girl!'

Marti tilted her damp face upwards, the tears in her

eyes adding a sparkling sheen to the glow of happiness in their emerald depths. 'Oh, Farrell! I love you so very, very much!' she breathed fervently on a partly sobbed note as his firmly etched mouth lowered to hers and their lips met in a sudden explosion of feeling that left her shaking with emotion when at last they parted.

'God, I've missed you!' he groaned thickly, burying his face in her hair, his arms keeping her crushed to him. 'I haven't been able to get you out of my mind since you left!'

'Nor I you,' she owned wistfully. 'Nothing seemed to hold any interest for me any more, except talking to Daddy about the Peninsula.' A rueful curve caught at the edges of her mouth. 'And all that did was to keep reminding me of you.'

'While I bought Leawarra in the hope that the extra work might help to banish you from my thoughts and my sleep,' he disclosed on a heavily expelled breath. 'And in that regard,' he drew back a little, his darkly framed eyes serious as they gazed into hers, 'there's still your feelings concerning the bush to be considered, isn't there, sweetheart?'

'Not really. Not any more.' Marti shook her head lightly, her eyes soft as they held his. 'I admit I had reservations myself for a long time as to whether I could successfully make the transition or not, or even if I really wanted to, if it comes to that, but I did mean what I said earlier about not being as uninterested as I made out, you know,' she tried to convince him on an urgent note.

'But why hide it in the first place?' His frowning expression was replaced by a wry one. 'It certainly would have made my position much more bearable if you hadn't. As it was, there didn't seem any point in revealing my feelings, let alone asking you to marry me.'

She hesitated, eyeing him shyly. 'Are you now?'

'Asking you to marry me?' He smiled slowly, an irresistible quality in the lazy curving of his lips making her feel weak all over. 'Uh-huh!' His voice deepened. 'If you'll have me.'

'Just try getting away!' she half laughed throatily, shakily.

Farrell's arms tightened about her convulsively. 'Not likely!' he vowed in gruff tones, his shapely mouth descending to cover hers in a long, consuming kiss that set the seal on their future.

'If only I'd admitted my growing interest in the life here, we might both have been spared a miserable couple of months,' Marti sighed in regret some minutes later, once her breathing had returned to normal.

'Although you still haven't explained why you kept it to yourself,' he reminded her, idly twisting a lock of her hair around his finger.

She stirred diffidently within his arms. 'Oh, it was for a mixture of reasons, I guess. Partly a reluctance to confess I'd been wrong condemning it out of hand in the first place. Partly in a misguided attempt to put some distance between us,' with a half-apologetic, half-bantering smile. 'But probably most of all because you'd made me feel so damned guilty about the way I'd behaved towards Daddy.' She cast him a ruefully chiding look. 'Did you really have to be quite so merciless in your denunciations?'

'Well, you *were* a thoroughly over-indulged brat, you know. And I had been requested to more or less— er—bring you back to earth, as it were,' he grinned impenitently. 'Besides, it also seemed a hopefully appropriate method for overcoming the dismaying attraction I found myself beginning to feel for that same very beautiful, but very aggravating brat. I'm afraid that right from the first moment of seeing you, you had an effect on me I neither expected nor wanted.'

'Well, I hope you're not expecting any sympathy from me,' Marti chuckled delightedly. 'Particularly in view of the fact that, in spite of your impossibly overbearing, condemnatory attitude, my senses waywardly wouldn't remain immune to you either.' Her lips formed an expressive moue.

Momentarily, Farrell's strong white teeth showed in a wide, captivating smile, and then his demeanour sobered somewhat. 'And because I wouldn't like that circumstance ever to change, I want you to know that I'll never object if you suddenly find yourself wanting to get away for a while, to return to the city for a few weeks,' he declared quietly. 'I'm used to the isolation and the lack of amenities and it doesn't bother me, but I do realise just how difficult it can be on someone who isn't accustomed to the life.'

'Oh, Farrell!' she murmured emotionally. 'Without you, the city just doesn't hold any attraction for me any more! This last couple of months proved that to me, if nothing else.'

He touched a hand to her cheek tenderly. 'As long as you don't sell the bush short, sweetheart,' he still warned. 'Because it is a hard life, even for those born to it, what with no radio or T.V. reception—our only contact with the outside world being by transceiver to the Flying Doctor Base, and a once-weekly mail-plane—cut off completely for months at a time during the wet, no theatres, restaurants, shops, nor even any neighbours, relatively speaking.' He appeared determined to divulge every shortcoming.

Refusing to be discouraged, Marti immediately quoted in return, 'But it does have you—most necessary, of course.' She added with a dimpling smile, 'A beautiful old house I have so many plans for, you just wouldn't believe; quite the prettiest outlook I've ever seen; not to mention masses of unpolluted air and waterways. The latter, so Daddy tells me, are literally brimming with barramundi southern anglers would give their right arm for an opportunity to catch, and much as it may come as a surprise, I thoroughly enjoy fishing. Then, of course there's no constant noise, and no legions of traffic either!' She gave an explicit grimace. 'I mean, the road up here may be, to coin a phrase, nothing short of atrocious, but you can at least keep moving while you're on it, which is more than can be said for the city's highways half the time.' Pausing, she gazed up at him half coaxingly, half apologetically. 'However, there is one change in the system I'd like to make, if you have no objections. I'd like to hire a cook-cum-housekeeper, if I could. Not only to ensure that, with all the work you'll apparently be doing, you do at least receive decent, edible meals, which could be extremely unlikely if I took on the role,' with a rueful grin, 'but also because I think I'd like to spend more time outside with you learning about the property. You never know, I may even reach the stage where I could actually be of some help to you.'

'You're that already, just be being here,' Farrell vouchsafed in husky tones.

This remark had Marti pressing closer to his muscular form. 'Is the idea acceptable, though?'

'Oh, I guess it could be arranged,' he drawled with lazy indulgence, his mouth curving in a heart-stirring smile. He raised a teasing brow. 'Anything else you have in mind?'

With her breath catching in her throat and her eyes darkening, she reached up to urge his dark head down to hers. 'Only this,' she averred in an ardent whisper, her lips already parting as his sensuous mouth closed on hers with a demand she was only too willing to answer.

Behind them, two figures appeared in the doorway, halted in surprise, and then smiling broadly at one another, quietly departed again. It was extremely doubtful that the two inside the room were even aware of the fact, however.

Here's how to get this special offer from Harlequin! As simple as 1...2...3!

January
BETTY NEELS
TREASURY EDITION
COUPON

1. **Each month, save one Treasury Edition coupon from your favorite Romance or Presents novel.**
2. **In four months you'll have saved four Treasury Edition coupons (only one coupon per month allowed).**
3. **Then all you have to do is fill out and return the order form provided, along with the four Treasury Edition coupons required and $2.95 for postage and handling.**

Mail to: Harlequin Reader Service

In the U.S.A.
901 Fuhrmann Blvd.
P.O. Box 1397
Buffalo, NY 14240

In Canada
P.O. Box 609
Fort Erie, Ontario
L2A 9Z9

BN-Jan-2

Please send me my Special copy of the Betty Neels Treasury Edition. I have enclosed the four Treasury Edition coupons required and $2.95 for postage and handling along with this order form. (Please Print)

NAME _____

ADDRESS _____

CITY _____

STATE/PROV. _____ ZIP/POSTAL CODE _____

SIGNATURE _____
This offer is limited to one order per household.

SUPPLIES LIMITED

This special Betty Neels offer expires
February 28, 1987.

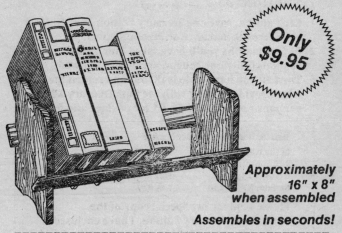